The Bonds of Dark Desire

Kevin Jobson

Table of Contents

Prologue

Wasn't this every girl's fantasy? Sam asked herself, trying to find the comic relief in the suspense they'd suddenly found themselves in. Sadly, any humor to be found in their situation withered away as the intensity of the stare-off between the two men increased.

What was a woman supposed to feel in this moment? Flattered? Impressed? No doubt some would feel objectified, simply because a girl shouldn't be some prize to be won.

But she liked being a prize. Deep down, there was something immensely satisfying in being coveted. Perhaps if there'd been no history or attachment, she may have even found it slightly arousing to have two men vying for her favor.

Instead, she felt nervous. It irritated her. She had curated a lifestyle in which to avoid complications...not to coax them out of hiding. Yet, when the past caught up to the present, bringing a 'mistake' and a 'carefree decision' to a crossroads, she guessed there was no escaping the consequences.

Blanche was standing at her side. Peculiarly, there was a lot less of her drink left than there was a moment ago. Everyone has their coping mechanisms when faced with an awkward moment. Blanche made hers clear with an empty glass that she held with such force that it threatened to shatter.

Samantha never needed many coping mechanisms, but she had to admit that the present moment would've felt a lot less awkward with a little inebriation well. Instead, her fingers twitched nervously at her side in anticipation of what either man was about to do next.

They didn't make a show of their power-play. Their assertion of dominance was fairly subtle. Around them, other people were in an entirely different microcosm and unaware of the primal stand-off happening right there in their midst.

Gareth didn't break eye contact as he moved closer to her. He placed his hand on her shoulder, squeezing it ever so gently to indicate his desire to leave. She didn't hesitate, turning around almost immediately to make her way to the exit by his side. But the eyes of another followed them, and she could feel that stare burning into her back.

She spared another look for Blanche, who seemed to noticeably unwind as they removed themselves from the equation of that suspense. She subtracted herself from the situation as well, slipping away the moment an opening presented itself. Yet, *she* wasn't the one who overwhelmed her attention. Against her better judgment, Sam also turned her gaze back at *him*, and the look in his eye told her that this saga of contesting desires was just about to begin...

Chapter 1:
Playtime Temptation

Samantha pushed her way through the pressing bodies and finally made it to the sky lounge.

As she took in the fresh air, she felt relieved to breathe out the smoke and sexual tension that arose on the dancefloor behind her. As the doors swung closed, muting the pulsating music and strobe lights, she felt the world around her settle.

She walked over to the balcony and leaned against it as she threw her head back to look up at the starstruck sky. The night swam around her, and every speck of light turned into a shooting star while her vision steadied itself after twirling around for the better part of an hour.

For anyone watching, it may have seemed peculiar, as if she just came out of a trance to step right into another rabbit hole. She was definitely high, but it wasn't on any kind of drug. She hated to admit it, but she knew it was the effect of this place. Its energy resonated with every molecule in her body. It was the people, their energy, and the thousand iridescent vapors that drifted among lustful intentions as a hundred people gave their bodies to the moment. She loved the feeling it sparked. Despite coming here a million times, she was delirious with happiness.

Dotted around the terrace, she saw the odd couple or gang mingling on a more chilled note. Talking, drinking, kissing…their states were varied, and she recognized each one as if she was a part of it.

Her life had been wild enough once upon a time. Maybe it still was.

The bartender eased himself into delivering the slow requests that trickled in. Everything was more relaxed, and she realized just once more how chaotic it really was back inside.

Samantha closed her eyes, opening herself to her other senses. The night breeze caressed her down her neck. Its touch was cool against her feverish skin, the heat of which emphasized the accents of the perfume that still clung to her. She had to laugh, feeling how everything still vibrated to the touch. The sky lounge was quiet. Nearly everyone was inside the club. Still, you could never entirely escape the beat that forced its way back into every cell. Her throat was dry. The hours had slipped away into the night, and she had nearly forgotten that they initially came out only to have a few drinks.

The 'few' turned into a bar tab. She didn't even know one could be opened on nights as busy as this.

The doors across from her burst open, and in crashed Blanche and Viola, laughing and hugging each other in the aftermath of the dancefloor euphoria.

"C'mon, Sam! You can't leave us hanging like that!" Viola teased, her dark curls crashing down in waves as she came to a stop next to her.

"God, no. I need a break, Vi," she returned. "I could jump out of this dress to cool down…"

"There's not much dress there," Blanche chimed in. "Are you sure you'll feel a difference?" she mocked, biting her lip to hold back a scoff.

"Hey!" Samantha playfully jibed at her friend's side to ward her off. Blanche burst out laughing. *Gingers*, she thought. *They really don't have souls.*

"She kind of has a point, hun," Viola said, "Those guys didn't pay us any attention before you came in. I'm pretty sure you have everything to do with attracting the wolf pack to gather around us. No wonder we had to push through. There was a ratio of four desperate males for every single girl in there."

"God, I'm not complaining!" Blanche bubbled. "All the handsome trust fund kids seem to be out. There are some choice hunters prowling back there in the woods. Hey Sam, maybe you could draw some of them closer to that table inside...."

"No. I'm not playing matchmaker tonight. Last time you woke up with two men in your flat, because you insisted on making 'friends' with twins. Needless to say, you still can't remember who was in the bed right next to you."

"Hey...it makes it easier to let the guy go," Blanche shrugged off.

"Then let's make sure you drag one home tonight to stay in practice!" Viola taunted, grabbing her by the hand to drag her back toward the madness inside.

"Stick with the fraternals this time!" Samantha shouted after her, shaking her head while laughing to herself. It was only a matter of time before she'd follow them; she knew herself all too well. As if feeling the impulse, she gripped onto the railing even tighter. Almost as if to keep herself in place.

"You look kind of relieved to be away from that..."

The voice came from her right, and she saw its owner standing off to the balcony's side. His attire was a simple white dress shirt that hung loosely over dark jeans and white high tops. It had quite a few buttons undone at the top and contrasted starkly with his golden-brown skin. A shard of onyx was strung around his neck, hanging neatly in the deep cleft of his chest. He wore dark-rimmed glasses that framed his face handsomely. It accentuated his features along with his dark, tousled hair. It took her a second to stop staring at him with such intensity to respond to his question.

"What gives you that impression?" she asked with a tone of amusement.

"Don't know," he smiled, "You look like a girl who wants to be both here and then not at all."

A laugh bubbled from her almost involuntarily. "How would you know what a girl like me wants?"

He shrugged, "Wild guesses to match wild people." There was a glint in his eye, or perhaps it was the way the light reflected off of his glasses. It was immediately striking as it paired with the way the corner of his mouth pulled up into a roguish half-smile.

She took in the smaller details as she stared at him. His jaw was strong and angular, juxtaposing with the softer look that came to rest on his face. The expression he wore was a mass of contradictions. Flecks of amber played innocently within light brown eyes, disarming her enough to almost fall for the sensual smile that locked away both secret and sin. He looked deceptively clever, deceptively innocent...and deceptively dangerous.

"I guess *you* look wild enough to take such a guess."

His head fell forward as he chuckled. He brought himself upright then, shuffling over to where she stood with hands in his pockets while looking at her over the rim of his glasses.

He reminded her of those aspiring collegiate professors that did not truly realize how attractive he was. He must be quite the sight in his collared shirt and pull-over kind of look. "So then, does that mean I'm right?"

Samantha sighed, for the first time really contemplating his earlier question. "I don't know. I've never really thought of it that way before. My life is fast-paced. Of late it's become a cycle of bouncing from one club to the other to completely exhaust my social budget while I'm young enough to do so. It becomes predictable when you look at it from the outside. But it's like a drug...on the inside, it's always thrilling and you go back for more."

"Well...that certainly got really deep. I was only expecting confessions like that on the second date."

"First of all, I've had enough to drink. Then...second date? What?" she guffawed, "Are you brazen enough to assume *this* is our first?"

"Could be. But we must establish a base first. What do I call you?" he asked.

"Unavailable," she teased.

"Aww, man. So I guess you're probably gonna let me head in alone then."

"Hmm. Probably. As you said, I'm a girl that doesn't seem to want to be here."

"So what if I head inside with the purpose of walking out the front door?"

"Depends. What's waiting for you beyond the exit?"

"Wouldn't you like to find out?"

She turned toward him, with a knowing look in her eye. "Perhaps after the second date," she said, walking back toward the bar.

"Is this the start of it?"

"Could be. Depends on whether or not you can guess my drink," she bit her lip as she said it, curious if he'd take the bait.

He kept her eyes locked with his stare, traipsing forward till he stood next to her at the counter.

"What can I get you guys?" the bartender asked.

"The lady looks like she might appreciate a Southern Comfort and lime. You can be generous with the ice."

"And for yourself?"

"A whisky on the rocks."

"Coming right up," the bartender acknowledged, turning around to work his magic.

"Nicely done," Samantha commented. "I like the touch with the ice. Wise move."

"I like to keep the drink diluted instead of the conversation," he answered coyly.

She scoffed. "Very chivalrous. I may already be drunk though."

"Nah. A drunk is never pretty, and you're gorgeous. You're still too beautiful to be anywhere close to looking smashed off your face."

"Oh my god. That was a very bad flirt..." she teased him, unable to hold back a smile.

He mirrored the reaction. "I think the honest ones are. They never really come out as you want them to. Then again, I wasn't trying to impress. I just wanted to see you smile."

She furrowed her brow in a gesture of mock disbelief, "Are you for real?"

"I'm a bit of an enigma actually."

"Oh really? Is that your friends call you?"

"They've settled with calling me Gareth," he offered.

The drinks arrived.

"Well," she started, picking up her glass while handing him his own, "glad we got to introductions so far into this thing."

"You still haven't introduced yourself, Samantha."

"My name is S—" she caught herself, figuring out what he had just done. "God. I may need a second of these sooner than I thought," she said, taking a big sip. "You knew all along? And still, you asked my name?"

"Actually, I just heard your friends calling you Sam. I just filled in the blanks. Looks like I was right."

"Perceptive."

"Not really. I just heard the aftermath of a bar tab calling your name. A cocktail does wonders to dial up the volume of the voice box."

He had a point there. Viola certainly was ahead of them on the drinks. You could tell whenever she gets louder. "Why do I get the feeling another bar tab is about to start right here?" Sam asked.

"That sounds more like an invitation than a question." He looked at her again with that quixotic expression on his face. She had known him for about five minutes, yet it somehow seemed to be the most familiar look to her in the world at that moment.

"A girl never makes a request—or asks a question—directly. It's better just to roll with whatever she is doing," Sam offered.

"Hmph. Last time I showed that kind of blind devotion to a girl I got myself in trouble."

"Ah, I see. We all trade in our warning labels to dress in something a bit more comfortable. Now you know!"

"Sure do. Probably missing even more of those red flags *right now*."

"You saying I'm dangerous?"

"Are you?" he countered.

"Immensely. I'd rethink this entire exchange right now." She took another long sip of her drink. "But...then again. I hope you're nothing like me..."

"To keep the conversation going?"

"Exactly."

"Damn. Did you just choose me over your friends? I thought they're waiting for you?"

"I don't choose my friends. They just seem to find me along the way, whether it's my way or theirs."

"Hmmm. Yeah, I can see that. You don't look like the type to find yourself following someone else's agenda."

"I did once when I was a young and starry-eyed little girl. Soon I found out that other people don't really have a sense of adventure."

"Adventure, huh? So you're a girl attracted to the notion of new experiences?"

"When you've had many of them, you're always looking for the next big thing to surprise you."

"I think that's impossible."

"What is?"

"To surprise you. I don't think anything gets past you," he hinted, taking a sip of his own drink.

"Expectations do. Disappointments follow."

"Whoa. Another one of those profound asides?"

"I have a few of them. You're lucky to have lived through two as it is..."

He bit his lip, ever so seductively as he regarded her. "So how can I convince a girl like you to continue sharing such deep philosophies?"

"Depends."

"Naturally. Do tell?"

"On how deep you want to get?" She was keeping her expression blank, yet secretly enjoying the playful exchange.

"Ha! Now see, I don't think you should ever ask a guy that kind of question."

"Scared it will be too rough a ride for you?" she teased.

He smirked, and his lids hovered hazily over his hazel eyes that gleamed with all kinds of secrets she wished she knew. "Are we...still talking of philosophies?"

"Philosophies can be about many things. *That* also depends..."

"Oh really? And what does *that* hinge off of?"

"What people want, of course."

"Hmmm, I see." He smiled to himself, staring down into his glass as his finger skimmed around the edge. "And what do *you* want, Sam?"

"I think I want to see if those feet work as fast as that mouth does." She took the last swig of her drink, slamming the glass on the table as she finished. "I want you to come dance with me." *Easy girl*, she chided herself. *Don't be brutish now.*

He chuckled. "I'm not really much of a dancer."

"Then you're not drinking enough, my friend." She picked up his glass, holding it up to him. "Liquid courage. Bottoms up."

He raised an eyebrow in mock skepticism, but accepted it and finished it off with a few gulps. Sam grabbed him by the arm, dragging him through the club doors and back into the chaotic thrum of trance music. The clubbers were going wild, and whatever they had taken was clearly showing its effects as the night had progressed.

The pair slipped between the raging crowds until they found themselves in a small gap between two groups of people. Samantha fell into the rhythm immediately. Gareth seemed out of place at first, not sure how to move his body to the hypnotic tracks. Eventually, he too, loosened up and a look of confusion turned into an elated expression.

Around them, the people were closing in, pinching the two of them closer and closer in that narrow space. Their bodies were touching then, flowing together and grinding as they allowed the music to take them.

"I'm not much of a dancer, huh?" she scoffed, echoing his previous comment loud enough for him to hear the remark over the din. She took a chance, folding her arms around his shoulders then, feeling how hot he was through the fabric of his shirt.

He placed his hands around her waist. She sensed how tentative he was, even tame. But amid that wildness, she experienced the gesture to be rather sensual as his hands landed feather-light on her body. He was a curious individual. Incredibly handsome, with a deceptive sense of inexperience about him. Yet, he seemed to know exactly what he was doing the more he moved.

She figured he was modest about his charms with a girl, and somehow that made him appealing in her eyes. He didn't realize how his casual and almost disheveled look carried a suave and sophistication about it. He couldn't know how his expressions, genuine and slightly animated, left a girl desperate for him to kiss her. He underestimated how the rolling tensions of his lithe body awakened powerful sensations in a woman that felt them up close. He was a primordial fire, and with each twist and gyration, Samantha could feel an age-old instinct consume her.

The music stopped suddenly, and momentarily doused the heat of the moment. The crowd was pressing in on them, and she dragged Gareth into one of the alcoves set into the wall on the side. Exhausted, they fell onto the chaise longue standing in the middle, breathless with elation.

"You do this every night don't you?"

She laughed, "I've definitely done this enough times."

"Do you leave all your partners this aroused?"

"It's the music talking, trust me."

"The music isn't playing right now..."

She turned to look at him then, genuinely taking him in. The way he was staring at her was probably the way any woman wanted to be looked at. She was no stranger to admiration. It had shone in the eyes of many men she came across, along with the glint of desire. That part wasn't absent in Gareth's eyes either, but there was something more. Perhaps it was the unabashed authenticity with which he made the comment while he shamelessly looked at her. From the start, she had felt as though he had been looking far deeper than just the surface. He saw more to her, and she thought it was the first time she felt visible that night. "Are you telling me you're turned on?"

His hand reached out, cupping her face. She didn't protest. Neither did she say anything as it moved to the back of her head, his fingers losing itself in her hair to draw her closer; so close, that she could feel the tingle of his breath rushing over her face. She expected him to kiss her then. She would have allowed it, welcomed it even. She was thirsty enough to be drowned in them.

He leaned in more, brushing his cheek past hers as he brought his lips to her ears. "I was about to ask you the same thing."

She shuddered in delight, and he noticed. He drew away from her then, slowly laying back into the many scatter cushions that dotted their seat. He looked happy with himself, with his incomplete seductions that left her on the edge of reason.

"My God, I think you're worse than I am," she commented.

He smiled in response but looked a little bemused. "How do you mean?"

"I thought I was a tease, but you coined the term."

"Chivalry isn't dead, remember..." The expression was cast with just enough mischief to drive her wild. He looked so untouchable then, as he stretched himself out and made himself comfortable.

"You look like someone who both wants to be here and someplace else entirely."

He laughed in response. "Using my own line against me, huh?"

"I altered it. You're restless, yearning...I see some of that in myself. Now I find myself tempted to say...that wherever you choose to go tonight, I hope you take me along."

She thought her words puzzled and both amused him. She didn't know how to place the look he gave her. It made her feel like she was some new discovery that he couldn't yet classify. But perhaps she was projecting. She was sure it was the look she gave him as well. He *was* an enigma, and she wanted to write her discoveries of his complexity all over her body.

"I wondered when you'd have another one of your profound moments," he said softly, loud enough only that she could hear.

"You stuck around long enough to listen," she answered in a near whisper.

Anything could have happened in that in-between space where they mutually teased their independent thoughts to some fantasy the other wasn't aware of. Samantha didn't know what she hoped for. Perhaps the next step, or the next great leap of uncertainty with someone exciting. Regardless of what romantic notions she entertained, they were all smashed to pieces in the anticlimactic moment when his phone rang.

His expression changed immediately as he reached in his pocket. He looked at the flashing screen, closing his eyes as if it left him uneasy to answer the call. "Look. I'm sorry for doing this. Just...give me a moment."

He stood up then, walking out of the alcove and through the throng of clubbers to find a more quiet space to talk. She lost sight of him soon as the bodies closed back in around the path he had opened.

Samantha's shoulders relaxed and she fell back, sighing. She didn't notice how tense the excitement and anticipation had made her feel. Foreboding crept into her mind as soon as he left, leaving her to wonder if she was not caught in some dream. She tried fighting against it, but the clarity of that moment alone made her doubt that serendipity could throw a guy like that so easily into her lap.

And make her want to jump on his lap in return.

A wild head of hair came peeking around the corner, and Viola grinned as she recognized Samantha before trotting over to plonk down beside her. "I see someone has been busy."

"Oh really," Sam challenged. "You're reading me now?"

"To filth, hun! No use denying it. The cheeks are flushed, and the hair is slightly more out of place since we left you. Not to mention the nerdy heartthrob that was just here. Yeah, we saw him." She looked around, scanning the crowd. "Speaking of, where'd he get off to?"

"God knows. He said he'd be back."

Viola swung around to face her. "He looked familiar, am I right?"

"He was stargazing outside. The sky lounge."

"Oh my God. That Adonis draped on the balcony? How did it go? A while back, it looked like you two were about to inhale one another. But your vibe is down. What happened?"

"I—I think I'm trying to figure it out myself, to be honest." She did sound a bit dejected. It was funny because she even remembered mentioning expectations and disappointments earlier on in the night.

Blanche came around the corner then, looking frazzled and then relieved to find her friends. "There you are! Honestly, why do we keep on playing Blind Man's Buff every time we head out? Can't we just stick together?"

"Adventure finds you when you venture off on your own, Blanche," Samantha said, putting her arm around the heart-faced little vixen that was her friend.

"Well, apparently...it also finds you when you lie in wait for it. That guy was hot! Damn. I think half the girls around us nearly orgasmed as he brushed by."

"Wow! TMI, Blanche," Viola commented.

"So, did something go wrong?" Blanche asked, ignoring the backlash.

"No, not at all. He's cool. He said he'd be a minute. You might even meet him," Sam said, winking at her.

Blanche looked confused, and something about that look made Sam's heart sink. "What? What happened?"

"It's just.... Sam, he walked out the entrance, and I saw him catching a cab outside."

She pressed her lips tight to avoid an expression forming on her face. *Typical.* But her mental comment didn't reflect how it really made her feel. She suppressed it as quickly as she could, before bursting out, "Time to get that tab active again. This calls for shots! Shots that flaking men are too fucking afraid to take!"

Chapter 2:
Choices

The next morning, Samantha woke with a dull ache in her head, a need for caffeine, and the mental carousel of bad choices.

She bolted upright as her eyes opened to the glaring mockery from the late morning sun, feeling around to affirm that the bedding was in fact her own. *There would be no walk of shame today.*

Relieved, she fell back into the pillows, immediately embraced by the recollections of the previous night. Or rather, an attempt to recall them. She felt lethargic. There was no doubt in her mind that it was going to be a slow morning. Luckily, it was a Saturday. She wouldn't have classified herself as hungover, but then again, she had acquainted herself with the feeling often enough that she sometimes wondered whether she hadn't developed a bit of a tolerance.

While playing with the images of glaring club lights and deafening music, her eyes fluttered shut again. She was ripped from her drowsy reverie when her phone started buzzing. The high pitch of the ringtone made her head throb, and she desperately groped for the device on her nightstand only to knock it under the bed.

Groaning, she nearly fell out of bed in an attempt to retrieve it on time while shrill ringing was only slightly muffled by the carpet. She flipped it around and swiped to answer without looking who had called.

"Hello?" she said half groggily, sounding like sandpaper being dragged across broken glass.

"Whoa, a voice that raw can only mean you've had some fresh meat."

It was Viola, with a tone of excitement that far exceeded Samantha's capacity to be receptive of her 'the morning after' interrogation. "God. Are we starting with sexual innuendos this early? I haven't even had my first cup of coffee."

"Well then, pop that pod in the machine, because you're about to give me a full recap. And don't you dare leave anything out."

Samantha didn't know where Viola's energy came from, especially since her friend had been far ahead of them in the drinks department the previous night.

"It isn't so much about me leaving anything out. The truth is, nothing actually happened."

"Uhm, I call bullshit."

"The sheets are empty my friend. Trust me, I've already felt around for anything odd poking around. No one-eyed snakes in this wilderness." *Thank God*, she thought.

"So, what happened to that German then? You know, the one after the nerdy heartthrob. I thought the two of you were hitting it off? I was sure he was going to be the rebound."

Samantha wished she knew. "Most men are wet tea bags, Vi. They fade in flavor pretty quickly. I don't think *he* was an exception."

"Hmm. Maybe you put him into hot water too long. Your interactions with steamy potentials are always a fine brew of intimidation. You've managed to disarm nearly every bachelor in this part of town with that quick mouth of yours."

"Sounds like you're saying that I scared the guy off."

"Well, did you?" The question was rhetorical, and Samantha knew it. "Listen. Gotta run. Please try and remember some more after you've pulled yourself together. Chat later!" The line went dead.

Sighing heavily, Samantha fell back into bed. *Did I?* She asked herself, obviously not thinking of the German. The question churned in her head, repeating itself a number of times, but it only succeeded in unchaining more confusion.

Deciding to be a productive member of society, she got up, dragged herself through a shower, and made her way downstairs to whip up a hearty breakfast. As the crunch of toast and smell of roasted coffee beans brought her closer to the edge of humanity, the subtleties of her exchange with Gareth started returning to her.

Gareth—the balcony-Casanova that had rendered her finest resistance useless. He had charmed her, lured her into a false sense of trust, and then left her without explanation.

The doorbell rang.

She froze midway through her breakfast with a mouth full of scrambled eggs. The doorbell sounded again, this time in a rapid succession of rings which made it very clear that her visitor was not about to leave.

Who in the hell—? she started to wonder, grabbing for a napkin to wipe at the corners of her mouth. She stood up and made her way to the front door. In the foyer, she caught sight of herself in the full-length mirror. Her look consisted of a crop top, denim shorts, wet hair, and heavy baggage under her eyes. Saturday morning fashions were developing a peculiar pattern of fusing her mismatched fashion sense with her Friday night decisions. Whoever managed to see her first the following morning undoubtedly had questions surrounding the story behind it all.

Reaching the front, she opened the door. On the threshold stood her mother, bearing the curdled look of disapproval on her features. "My god. It's alive."

Samantha delved in the deepest parts of herself for a semblance of divine strength. "It's good to see you too, Mother."

"Oh there's no need for pleasantries, dear," her mother said, shouldering past her to step inside the house. "I know you practically despise these visits from me when unannounced. You do so hate being caught with your skirt down." She was looking around, trying to pinpoint the many things around the home she would address Samantha on later.

"Like mother, like daughter. After all, it all started for me when your skirt was around your knees."

"Your father was tasked with getting past a pair of bell-bottoms. In my day, a woman made it a challenge." Her eyes came back to rest on her daughter—the scrupulous eyes of Daphne Claremont.

She had cut many a man down with those sharp eyes in her day. She did it with her husband as well. She tried it with her daughter, finding only that she too had acquired the unique talent to make men quake in their boots. "God, you really do look like death warmed up. I don't know how we're going to be on time before your father's friends arrive."

"Wait...what?"

"It's the last Saturday of the month dear. Your father is hosting the brunch club again."

"Mother. I've told you once before that I won't be attending those any longer," Sam answered seriously.

"Which is all good and well. I've grown bored of the same crowd myself. The same gossip does become tedious. But you did happen to commit to this one a while ago. So there is no backing out at this point."

"Why would I commit to sipping on mimosas at an elderly white party?" Samantha countered.

"Because said party will be attended by Fae Mayweather, editor in chief of *Fashion Digest*."

"Fuck!" Samantha exclaimed, running her hand over her face. "It completely slipped my mind."

"I thought so. I had expected you to be dressed already. But you've clearly been going through a phase, so I thought I'd intervene and come tell you to pull your head out of your ass. It's not a hat. You should be designing them instead. I've just finished my morning run and I was about to head back to the estate. It's clear, however, that you need some help."

"Mom, I'm curious. Does the club entertain the use of such crude language in their circles?" she asked sarcastically.

"We *are* the club, dear. It entertains whatever show I choose to throw. Now, you best get dressed."

"I'll have to look through my closet for—"

Her mother reached into the bag she was carrying, pulling out a plain sky-blue dress. "I already have your outfit. I'll dig through your accessories to complete the ensemble while you make the rest of yourself presentable." With that, her mother marched to her bedroom. Samantha following right behind.

"Isn't that a bit presumptuous? To choose a dress to wear for your fashion photographer daughter?"

"The item is from one of your shoots a few weeks ago. This is a strategy, my dear. You cannot hope to impress by going in your questionable selection of boho chic. Fae is a fashion columnist. She's not a curator of backyard sale clothing. How you choose to dress for work is your prerogative. How you *present* your work is mine."

"Well, sorry mother. I didn't realize this was a shared career path."

"Everything in this family is shared. Objectives, strategies, tactics, and achievements. We're building on a legacy, dear. It is paramount that you are aware of the constituents thereof, as well as your contribution."

Another Saturday, another Claremont initiative. Samantha had forgotten just how well-oiled that machine was. She always prided herself in having separated most of her achievements from the family agenda, but ironically, they always seemed to align perfectly to the Claremont image. When you had a daughter who gained public notoriety with her career, it was effortless to have the family name ride on her success. And so her job had become the fulcrum to a continued confirmation bias. Another Claremont once again establishes herself in a position of influence.

Her mother would never let it go. Her father...well, she wondered if he had even noticed. Tom Claremont had established his empire and achieved everything he set out to do already. Did he really care anymore, or was he just enjoying the spoils of war?

Reaching the bedroom, Samantha dove for the vanity desk. She fished out a nude eyeshadow palette, a light bronzer, and discarded about five bullet applicators of old lipstick in the process. She hated these artificial glow-ups. It made her feel self-conscious and uncomfortable, but she knew a woman like Fae appreciated the artistry involved.

"So..."

God. It's starting already. Her mother had taken *that* tone again. It was the type of voice that left you with a mixture of bated breath and anxious anticipation. Her mother could throw any kind of curveball with that voice. She always had the quirk to open a conversation like that, as if she had assumed her daughter should already have opened it by now. "Yes...?"

"What's his name?"

"Whose name?" she asked, knowing full well whom she was referring to.

"Come now. No need to be coy. You're about three insults behind since I arrived, and I know of nothing else but a man that could leave you so disarmed."

Her mother stood behind her while Sam sat in front of the vanity mirror. She was hardly surprised by the quick read on the situation. Not only was she the spitting image of the woman, but she also matched her personality. Often, Samantha had wondered whether it was the reason for their regular clashes. Being like her daughter, Daphne Claremont naturally knew her all too well.

As a result, a mixture of behavioral cues must have given her away. *Of course, she knew*, Samantha thought. *She knew the signs.* Daphne had been like her daughter once, and that made her far more attentive to certain details.

"It's nothing. It's a silly little flirtation that did not end up going the way that I had I planned." Sam tried to keep her tone neutral, but there was more than a hint that she was left bothered by Gareth's sudden disappearance.

"If it was a silly little flirtation, then you'd have been on time this morning."

"No need to chide me on the things I know already, mother."

"I'm not chiding. I'm merely giving perspective. Best you get it soon to avoid any distractions when discussing business." Sam knew her mother must have meant well, but the woman was such a tactful know-it-all that the good intentions seem to be lost.

"I can handle Fae."

"Fae doesn't get handled. *She* handles things herself. It's a fine distinction she learned to make when working in a male-dominated echelon of visionaries. Objective as she is—or claims to be—you'll find that she'll be taking measure of you through your entire first conversation."

Samantha sighed and took a deep breath to steady her temper. "I know, mother. I've done this before..."

"Indeed. But your mind wasn't on some man."

"This man you keep referring to...is inconsequential. Of that, I can assure you. I know you'd like to think that you're warning me of being unwary, but I am well ahead of you." She beat the make-up brush against her skin, going in harder with every word that supported what she willed herself to believe.

The truth, however, was that Gareth had been on her mind for most of the morning, and for the better part of the night since he left her without a word—even as she'd been looking for some other distraction. Her mother was right. Her laser focus gave her actions precision and lethality. She didn't allow herself to be dissuaded from her motives. Not by anyone. But inadvertently she had opened herself enough to feel disappointed.

It made him stand out among the many others who had tried to woo her. He was different from her usual type, more quick-witted, and full of surprises. Beyond that, they had tested the surface tension of their attractions a couple of times through the course of the night.

But some part of her had clearly seen a connection where he hadn't. For a moment she had made herself vulnerable, only to have him vanish without a trace.

"Fine, then. If you say so. I'm not wholly convinced, but we don't have much time to debate the issue at present. I am going to grab your pearls to go with this. It should round the look off nicely."

"Don't forget to take a string of them for yourself. You'll probably need something to clutch onto when I embarrass you."

"No need to be snide, Samantha. You know I only have your best interests at heart," she prowled off to raid the closet.

Right. Because my interests are undoubtedly the Claremont agenda for preserving family pride over personal well-being. After applying the finishing touches, Sam looked herself over.

Elegant to a fault...perhaps a touch wild...

Her dark blonde hair fell in naturally large ringlets around her face, and she debated whether there was any time to straighten and plait it. With some help, her complexion had a bit more warmth to offset the cool of her blue eyes. She noticed other small details in the reflection, but the one thing that lured her attention was the absence of the steely resolve that normally gleaned in her eye.

In a few moments, she would play the great pretender—a powerful legacy of the Claremont family line. But deep down she felt like a simple girl who was battling with a feeling that hadn't stirred inside of her in a long time.

***

The brunch was another colossal waste of money.

Over-catered and over-boozed, the event proved to be nothing but a pompous gathering of the business elite of the city. When she was younger, Samantha found herself entertaining the Saturday gatherings. But the appeal grew old very quickly; however, it did have its perks.

One of them was the pursuit of potential business ventures with her parents' rich friends. Fae Mayweather was such an individual. Life had pieced her together from failed marriages, wine, and resounding success in her publishing company. Her soul was made of ice and the adoration from others, and no one could help but respect the formidable woman once they were confronted with her.

Samantha respected her, but not out of fear. She could appreciate Fae's indifference in the face of bullshit, and her lack of tolerance for the egotistical peacocks that pranced around the company they believed they equally compared to.

On meeting, Fae noticed these qualities, and if Samantha didn't know any better she would have said that the woman actually liked her. When confidence meets its equal on the playing field, it was like finding a friend amid a sea of strangers. Both Sam and Fae were fully aware of their potential and capabilities and saw eye to eye almost immediately despite the years and experiences that lay in the chasm of differences between them.

The conversation lasted less than fifteen minutes, and Sam was promised a meeting with the editorial team of *Fashion Digest* on the coming Monday.

Her mother was no stranger to the feeling of self-assurance either, but because of some vicarious fantasies she was living out through her daughter, Sam found her nervously winding between guests in a false display of being in social demand.

"Oh, thank God! You made it. Fae has been here for a good hour."

"She'll be here for a couple more by the looks of it. For women, parties like these are like golf days for men. She is making money with every mimosa she finishes. And she's driving away in a sedan instead of a golf cart after victory."

Daphne beamed with approval. "You spoke to her then. Good girl. You have that afterglow of corporate negotiation. My guess is that it reaped benefits?"

"You can add a few pages of next month's issue to your daughter's scrapbook." Fae envisioned an entire spread for the Fall collection. If Sam could attest to anything regarding Fae Mayweather's character, was that her vision usually saw fulfillment.

"Excellent." Noticeably pleased, her mother immediately assumed the guise of hostess. "Well, I need to mingle. I'm proud of you, Samantha." Daphne placed a hand of cold affection on her daughter's soldier before disappearing among the crowd in the estate gardens.

"Of course you'd be," Sam said to herself when her mother was out of earshot. A butler came past bearing a drinks tray, and by compulsion, she stopped him to down a glass of champagne before giving him a curt smile and walking away. The last look he gave her was something of a mix between disapproval and fascination. He was clearly not used to that kind of behavior.

Samantha decided to make a getaway, so she might spend her Saturday in ways that did not involve copious drinking to deal with her mother and their snobbish social circle.

The tea garden of the Claremont estate spanned across a great lawn that almost touched the sea if a beach and road didn't stand between them. They were in East Hampton. It wasn't converted into anything of significance to entertain the hobbies of the upper class, aside from the hosting of large parties. In fact, that was its defining feature. The estate ground was always filled with people. The larger the party, the more intimate the event. The more people that attended increased the chances of running into someone you knew. And the more people who happened to see you was equivalent to maintaining your status. One could never blend into the background with large parties. It made them notoriously difficult to escape as well.

She moved between a congested crowd of people near the back entrance of the mansion, nudging her way through perfumed trophy wives and the sharp cologne of their husbands. For a brief second her movement between them had been unhindered, causing her to move with such speed that her collision with a tall body nearly sent her sprawling backward.

For a moment her temper flared but was snuffed out just as she looked up into Gareth's face. Startled at first, he went ashen immediately, turning scarlet as recognition dawned on his face. If Samantha had been any less versed in dealing with awkward confrontations, she would have felt her cheeks burning with a similar kind of self-awareness. But she had been around the block and had dealt with a number of men who had ghosted her.

"Sam?" he said incredulously. "What are you doing here?"

"Now, that's the kind of small talk that won't really help in making anything less uncomfortable for you."

"I—I just didn't expect to see you here."

God, he was handsome, even though guilt wasn't entirely his look. She cursed herself for even having the thought.

"Of course you didn't. You probably wouldn't have been around otherwise." In her own mind, Sam was berating herself for the hint of anger that rode her tone as she addressed him. It meant that she allowed his disappearance to affect her, and she prided herself in not being held back by the faults of other men.

"Sam…I meant to reach out to you. I just—"

"Lacked a sense of moral decency?"

"Listen—" he started, looking around anxiously as their conversation started to draw attention. "Let's talk in private, please. I *want* to explain myself, but I need you to give me a chance by calming down."

Samantha hated to be dimmed down or muted, and a part of her longed to be reactive in answer. However, she was always a social tactician. She, like everyone at that party, knew better than to flaunt their personal drama in full display. She brought her voice down to a whisper, "First of all, telling an angry person to calm down is expecting gasoline to douse a fire. Secondly, it's a big fucking liberty to ask for a chance when the time frame for being considerate has long expired. What the hell are you even doing here?"

"I was—" he sighed before rephrasing, "My boss. He arranged for me to be here."

"You work for one of these men?"

"No. He couldn't make it. I'm representing him. However, he arranged for me to come and meet a collegiate fellow that acted as his mentor back when he was in university. It opened up the doors to his own success, and he hopes it could secure a postdoctoral opportunity for me abroad."

"Abroad, huh? So...you *never* intended to reach out then. I was your plaything for a single night that you could engage and discard at the same time to avoid any complications."

"Sam. That's hardly fair. You can't bind me to such a derailed rationalization. I—"

"Save it. Pro-tip, don't give a girl a lead to go on if it is only meant to lead her astray." She started to walk past him.

He grabbed her by the wrist then, in an attempt to stop her.

"Let go of me!" she breathed in a vicious whisper.

Her words struck hard, and he flinched, looking like an animal that had been whipped into submission. His grip wasn't hard and conveyed nothing but a silent plea for understanding. But she was not open to receiving it. As soon as he freed her, she turned around and kept on walking.

All the while, she knew his eyes were following her. She was not unfamiliar with the sensation, having been in this position before. Yet, in taking stock of her emotions, she knew the run-in with Gareth had affected her more than she was willing to admit. She wouldn't show any of it here though. Her exit through the estate was quick, yet methodical. She needed to get out and escape the prying eyes that might have caught even a slither of their confrontation.

She stalked through the corridors of her childhood home, at once unnerved and unwelcome among the adornments that she should have been used to after years of living there. But the affluence, the space, the grandeur of it all...it all left her hollow and uncomfortable. She yearned for the enclosed comfort of her own home. She longed for its less imposing scale, its simplicity, and the safety it offered to deal with her confusion.

Still, she couldn't fathom that she was so riled up by one man. The thought confronted her anew as she made it to the driver's seat of her one car. *Dammit, Claremont. Why did you allow yourself to be vulnerable? Why did you allow yourself to buy into meaningless charm? Have you learned nothing?*

She exhaled heavily, letting her head fall back as a feeling of calm settled over her. *Come now. Don't let your mother be right about you. You're the captain of your own ship. So what? You allowed a small wave to rock you.*

"One man. One miscalculation. One disappointment. A hundred lessons." She said it out loud, increasing the affirmative power of her self-styled mantra. *But was it just the one man?*

The question willed itself into her mind without warning, and she knew there was more to the fervent reaction that she displayed mere minutes ago. It was the culture of megalomaniacs, the exclusivity, and the disingenuous interest of the circles she moved in. It inadvertently attracts a type: men of a certain disinterested caliber and women with a predisposition to entertain themselves in the ubiquitous trivialities of the upper class.

She turned the key in the ignition and as the engine roared to life, she felt herself reclaim her power. She drove away from it all and reminded herself why she left in the first place...while trying to forget why she returned.

Chapter 3:
New Toys

"Erm...what are you doing?"

"Trying to get some color," Blanche drawled, sinking deeper into the deck chair to make herself comfy.

Viola looked skeptical, even while wearing shades. "Blanche, honey, *red* is *not* your color. You might want to put on some sunscreen."

"I'll be absolutely fine," Blanche responded lazily.

"So said a million gingers who came before you. I don't think skin tone is supposed to clash with one's hair," Viola persisted.

"You know...now *that's* a conversation we can have," she said in that tone of mock seriousness, taking her sunglasses off for emphasis. "The blatant discrimination of my people."

"You want to talk about the plight of redheads?" Samantha asked, peeking beneath her sunhat at her friend.

"Not the plight. The *struggle*!" Blanche pointed out.

"We're talking about that struggle *right now*, hun," Viola said. "Redheads and UV rays just don't gel well—it's a losing battle. "Let's not make melanoma part of the protest."

"Geez, no sympathy for the oppressed," Samantha said, sighing before settling back into her sunbathing position. "Guess there's no point pushing narratives with a beach blonde and a Greek."

"Beach blonde?" Samantha exclaimed. "Listen here...I'm hardly a Baywatch pin-up."

"God, from the way some guys were staring at your bust the other night, I'd say you'd give Pamela a good run for her money," Viola commented. If it had been anyone else but her friend, the comment would have come across as snarky.

"Damn. Did you get here late because you sharpened your tongue at home?" Sam countered.

"I think I overdid it last night with the drinks. I'm still developing a personality."

"You mean to tell us that your flavor of 'bitch' this morning is because of clubbing two nights ago?" Blanche asked from the side.

"Oh no. I got over that real quick. Tyrone and I just had some friends over for games last night. We went a bit heavy on cheap wine. His buddy said he was bringing over some 'juice boxes.' The kids happened to be around when he was chatting on the phone."

"Hmm. Don't know how wise it is for you to be in direct sun then," Samantha remarked.

"Ah. Bless cheap wine," Blanche chipped in. "Really gets you closer to where you need to be a lot sooner."

"You mean smashed off your face? Pfft. What do you know of cheap wines anyway? Your entire cabinet is stocked with vintage reds," Samantha challenged.

"I dabbled once—in cheap wine, cheap conversations, and cheap guys," Blanche said with a hint of whimsy riding on her voice.

"All guys are cheap, girls. Every one of them," Samantha said, stretching out on her own deck chair as she looked out over the Hampton beachfront. Blanche struck it lucky with a modest—by Hampton standards—beach house cottage originally built as an add-on to a larger estate. When the owners were selling, she was the first to find out. On gorgeous days like this, it really paid off to have friends that had houses with a view.

"I beg to differ. That tall drink of water the other night looked as though he was making you thirsty," Viola giggled, seeming more capable of some personality than she had given herself credit for.

"Too bad he left me parched after one sip."

"He never called? Never looked you up? Are we...talking about the hot nerd or the German?"

"Who is this damn German you keep referring to?" Sam asked while laughing. "He was a Dane. And no, it was the naughty scholar. He never took my number. Neither of us thought of that. Then again, I thought he was coming back after he walked outside to take the call."

"Rookie move, my friend..." Viola remarked snidely.

"Oh please!" Sam exclaimed. "You've been out of the dating game so long you forgot what it's like. You can't be a rookie when you're flirting with a flake from the start. Besides. I did see the ass yesterday, at my parent's Saturday social."

Both Viola and Blanche bolted upright, their attention sparked. "You're only telling us this now?" Blanche asked, looking starved for the details.

"It didn't seem important. He's just another douchebag that spun a story to negate his shortfalls."

"What the hell did he do at your parent's gig?" Viola suddenly seemed over her hangover.

"I didn't ask. I was too pissed, to be honest. He plays evasion tactics the night before, and then I find him at my parent's brunch club. I mean, what are the chances, right? The whole thing just seems so apathetic on his part. Like he didn't care. Life just went on. Anything he does can be ok, as long as he can continue living it up."

"Did he try to explain?" Blanche asked.

"I didn't give him a chance."

"Sam!"

"Don't 'Sam' me with that tone of voice! I'm damn tired of men who take liberties."

"He doesn't sound like a user. I mean, you didn't sleep together, there was no date whatsoever. I don't think you even kissed that night. Normally a player gets something from a girl before he just moves on."

"He did. He actually had a chance and he blew it," Samantha responded.

"Whoa!" Blanche exclaimed. "Are you telling me you *digged* him?" She smiled mischievously. "You're like the most unapproachable bachelorette of East Manhattan. Men spill their drinks nervously long before they have the chance to down it for some courage, knowing that they're gonna talk to you. I was impressed that this guy even took a shot."

"And now," Viola continued, "You're telling us that he conquered you?"

"Ok, listen. You two are trying to read between the lines on a blank page. It was flirtation on the dance floor. Nothing more."

"Doesn't look like it." Viola was clearly enjoying the new bits of information. She had the tendency to be a real abrasive bitch that could rub you the wrong way if you let your guard down. Sam loved the girl, but her friend was one of the few people who could really grate her tits.

"Ok. Enough. I call a ceasefire. Granted, I allowed myself to get a little carried away by a guy and I'm still a bit peeved that he was ballsy enough to leave me stranded after that encounter."

"What was it like?" Blanche asked with feverish curiosity. "We were trying to see through people, smoke, and laser light to where you were sitting. We only caught glimpses."

She would never forget the feeling. Her last few minutes with Gareth were an edge-of-your-seat type of encounter that left her hot and bothered for hours after. "Intense. Yeah...that's a good word."

"Ok, ladies. Here's what we're going to do," Viola declared, lying back down on the deckchair, with her orange summer dress billowing around her ankles to add to the drama. "Sam here needs a warm bed for a night, so we're going to find this Gareth and start plotting our next move. We have the entire workweek. We need a surname, occupation, and any tea we can get our hands on. The more piping hot, the better."

"You have fun with that. For your information, I actually have a busy line-up this week and will definitely not waste my energy on a guy I checked out under club lights and loosened inhibitions."

"Oh, I will. Trust me. And when you're replacing bed posts after a sweaty all-nighter, I expect a thank you. Send the bill too...I don't mind paying."

***

The next Friday came like a sigh of relief as Samantha walked into her house. Meredith's narrowed eyes greeted her while she perched on the backrest of the sofa. The Siamese was as aloof as ever, offering a glare of judgment and silent reprimand for being left alone the entire day.

Samantha sagged against the nearest wall as she threw down her bags, feeling exhausted. She met Meredith in the stare-off. "You're not one for much sympathy are you?"

The cat just kept on looking at her.

"Not one to talk much, huh? Been discussing the state of world affairs with your neighbors no doubt. That can really exhaust a girl. C'mon, maybe a meal will make you feel better."

In the ultimate gesture of cold indifference, Meredith simply turned her head to the front again and closed her eyes.

"Bitch." Samantha dragged herself upright, making her way upstairs. She slipped out of her business attire and the day's problems and unwound her tense muscles under a hot shower.

The deal she struck with Fae Mayweather yielded a contracted partnership for the Fall shoot of the magazine. Little did she know that the fashion mogul was a slavedriver. Meeting upon meeting had been scheduled with designers, editors, and columnists to establish the near militant game-plan for the photo segments that would accompany it. No sooner had decisions been made, than they were executed. The shoots had started immediately. In the height of summer, Fae wanted the Fall preparations to be a pristine passion project that was birthed early and then nurtured until the day of release. Her recipe for success was indisputable, but it proved to be akin to perfectionist warfare.

The mere thought of the busy week ahead of her made Sam ravenous. She made her way down to the kitchen. What met her was an empty pantry, a fridge filled with old condiments, and a bag of chips in one of the cupboards. A week spent eating catered meals prepared by the local vegan delis had made her lax in doing some shopping. Long term team projects had their perks, but also their costs.

After more searching, she found a lonely, discarded frozen dinner in the abyss of her freezer. At that point, anything looked appetizing, and two minutes later she found herself in front of the microwave watching her least favorite episode of the defrost setting while leaning against her kitchen counter.

She also remembered to feed Meredith.

The girls invited her for movie night, but work commitments made her decline. She didn't even contemplate letting them know that she'd been let off sooner, yearning for an uneventful night at home.

She scarfed down her meal in the kitchen, not bothering with plating, ceremony, or anything that'd require effort. The meal hardly touched the sides of her stomach, and afterward, she still felt unsatisfied by the anticlimactic turnout of her expectations of the night. Against sound judgment, she snatched the bag of chips as well. Hidden away in a corner of a top cupboard, she also found an unopened jar of Nutella. She was having the 1st world version of a poor woman's feast tonight.

Treasures secured, she made her way to the living room where she made one of the highback chairs her throne. The crisps were stale and the Nutella tasted like guilt with every spoon, and try as she might, she just couldn't be gratified by the hollow promise a night alone had afforded her.

Many such evenings usually passed with idle thought and little need to get lost in anything profound. Series hopping through Netflix helped that process along. But on that fateful Friday, Samantha Claremont found herself sitting in absolute silence as contemplations were her only company along with a stand-offish feline. Her mind took her everywhere from her career, her friends, her family...and to a past life that was so very different from the one she was living right now.

A hard rapping on the front door snapped her out of her reverie, and she had to wait and listen to be sure she hadn't hallucinated. It came again, morphing into an incessant pounding that even had her cat direct an alert stare toward the front door.

Who the hell could that be? She certainly hadn't been expecting anyone, and she couldn't remember the last time anyone came knocking on her front door.

The knocking came again, this time an irregular sequence of beats, some of which almost seemed by accident. She stood up, realizing that she was once again not dressed for any surprise company. Her front door didn't even have a peephole, and she realized that her porch lights weren't switched on to spot her nighttime visitor through a window. Despite an overriding sense of caution, she still found her hand reaching out to turn the handle. The door swung open just as another knock landed. A flailing arm shot through, caught in the motion, and when the person at the door regained his balance, the indoor lights shone onto Gareth's face.

A mixture of emotions must have played on her features then. Shock, irritation, amusement—she felt all those things distinctly and then at once as she looked at the swaying frame of the swoon-worthy night-club animal on her threshold. "Now this is certainly unexpected," she got out in what sounded to be a near ragged whisper.

He flashed her a beaming smile. He was happy. Too happy. The kind of happiness that you only get from a night of mixing recreational substances.

***

"C'mon, c'mon. Pick up..." Sam got edgy as the fifth ring passed without response until someone finally took the call.

"Hello?"

"What the hell, Vi. I just texted you. What, did you drop the phone and run away when I called?"

"Um, well, excuse me for not jumping at the very instant you decided to invite an issue into your life," she responded sarcastically. *"I don't get why you didn't just turn him away."*

"Did you even read the damn message? It's not that sim—Wait, just hold on a sec," Samantha said, holding her hand over the phone. "Hey, hey, hey! Don't touch that! What do you think this is, an interactive play exhibit? Sit the fuck down, please."

"Geez, sorry," Gareth said, putting down the delicate mantelpiece ornament he'd been inspecting.

"Thank you," she said, removing her hand from the receiver. "Yeah, so, please tell me what to do."

"What do you mean I should tell you what to do? This isn't my mess!"

"Come again? If I'm not mistaken, you were super keen on finding this thing that's now strutting around my house. From what I gathered, your little investigation raised questions with a friend of a friend of *another* friend...whom I happened to have stood up. Because of some twisted little revenge ploy and unresolved feelings, this guy gave Gareth my address. You must have known there'd be some kind of consequences."

"Sam, I don't get what the big issue is. You said he rolled up to your house after having a good night. So what? He's a hot guy that's high off his rocker and perhaps a little bit tipsy. It will wear off. Boom! Problem solved. Why didn't you just close the door if you were so averse to having him there in the first place?"

"I did. Then he climbed through one of my spare room windows."

"He did what now? How?"

"He jumped from a branch."

"Alright, listen. You're not making any sense. There's no way he could j—" The line went quiet, but Samantha could still hear breathing on the other end. She leaned against the door, curling a lock of hair around her fingers as she waited for her friend to

come to the conclusion. *"Wait, is he a friend of **that** friend who always carried around his pouch of 'magic'?"*

"That's the one."

"For Christ's sake, Sam. That guy carried so many mushrooms he could start his own produce aisle. What the hell did you do to upset him that he'd send Gareth your way with his third eye opened?"

"How was I supposed to know those two would even get to start talking? No one gave me the run-down on the shit men get up to when they do hallucinogens," Sam said sheepishly.

"And the window? You live by yourself. Don't you ever do a routine lockdown at night?" Viola asked, sounding exasperated.

"Can we just reiterate that my window is on the second floor and that he swung from a damn branch to get to it? I'm not a talent scout. His acrobatics caught even me off guard. I just heard a loud thump and groan coming from upstairs, and there he was..."

"Why didn't you just kick him to the curb after that?"

"Because he parked so deep on the sidewalk that his wheel nearly touched my front porch. You want me to send a guy like that driving during this hour? I don't even know how he made it all the way here unscathed! Look. Despite my reservations, he isn't a bad guy. I can't allow one interaction to dictate how I treat him when he clearly needs some help."

"Girl, it sounds like you're trying to push the responsibility of offering that help onto someone else."

"Sharing is caring."

Viola sighed. *"Listen, Sam, try to reframe your position here for a second. You know what just happened, right?"*

"Uh…yeah. Kind of the reason I'm calling you. Your exploits as a sleuth snowballed into a man pitching up at my doorstep in the dead of night to have a serious talk…that we still haven't got to, because he's looking for fairies behind houseplants."

Viola was silent for a moment, *"Well, now you're making me feel bad…"* Viola said in a tone of playful exasperation.

"Yeah. That was kind of the point of calling you too," Sam said, unable to keep herself from laughing at the situation a little.

"Ok. Calm down. What I meant to get to is this: you've got a steamy little lost boy wobbling around in your house, whose inhibitions are probably so loose by now that he could start his own harem. Don't you think this is, I don't know, opportunity knocking at your door?" Viola nudged naughtily.

"Oh—my—God! You're not actually suggesting I take advantage of him are you?" Samantha responded in disbelief.

*"Oh, honey. If a man rocks up to **your** door having **looked** for you, then anything after that is pure happenstance."* Samantha could just imagine Viola sitting on the edge of her bed, looking smug as if she offered the most sage advice in the world.

"Alright smartass," Sam giggled. "So, c'mon. Help a girl out. How do I get rid of him?"

"You don't," Viola answered matter-of-factly.

"Say what now?" Sam asked, unsure if she misheard. "What do you mean? What am I supposed to do?"

"Take responsibility."

"There's a hallucinating frat boy having heightened experiences around a palette color scheme and minimalist furniture and you want me to handle it. God forbid he says anything more transcendental. He may just lose the plot entirely!"

"Sam, he's past his mid-20s. He's a postdoc with a stable job and despite the odd gaming and fandom obsession, he's actually pretty mature. You got off easy, my friend. You should have seen Tyrone after his first magic mushroom. I needed to use the handcuffs to keep him tied to the bed."

"What were you doing with handc—" Samantha didn't finish her question, remembering Viola's occasional fetish with voyeurism. "Never mind."

"Just chill and have some fun with it."

"No. Let's get something straight. I don't take responsibility for other people. I don't heal, I don't coddle, and I certainly don't play the parent," Samantha said more sternly.

"You just did, at the very moment you allowed him to stay."

"So that's it. You're just going to leave me alone with this?" Sam asked incredulously.

"Sam, I love you. But I'm doing you a favor. You're a career woman whose handle in life is creativity. So...H-A-N-D-L-E it! You've got all the skills to get down to business. And I'm not talking Saturday morning mimosas and networking. "

Suddenly, everything was way too quiet.

"Oh...shit."

"What? What happened?"

"I think I lost him. Dammit! I hope he's somewhere in the house."

"Why don't you—"

"Listen, I'll message later."

"Have fun!" Viola shouted before Sam cut the call short, perhaps deliberately and with some irritation.

Her unwanted guest was nowhere to be seen. Meredith came skulking around the corner of the couch, surveying her surroundings before venturing tentatively in the open. Gareth had done the near-impossible by picking Meredith up earlier. It baffled Sam that the cat even liked it, let alone tolerated it. But when Gareth got a bit too absorbed in the surplus of love and looked about ready to lick her, Meredith was spooked. She promptly squeezed herself out of his grip, nearly tearing the arm of his shirt, and dashed behind the furniture.

It didn't take her long to hear scuttling upstairs. Another crash and tumble confirmed her suspicion of where he was. She sighed heavily, dragging herself in pursuit.

At first, she was unable to find him. Amazingly, evidenced by either an open door or something that had been knocked over, he had made his way into every room. Samantha couldn't remember that she ever dealt with someone who had played around with magic mushrooms. More so, she doubted that she ever even heard of someone being drunk to add to the mix. Eventually, the creak of floorboards guided her in the right direction.

Moving in, the house had a quaint little charm that she wanted to make use of. The placement of the master bedroom didn't agree with her though, so she decided to get creative. The result was the conversion of the attic into her bedroom, leaving the original bedroom open to be remodeled into a walk-in closet. It was every girl's dream who had half a fashion sense to invest in.

Sure enough, she found him trying to open the slanted attic window while attempting to get out at the same time. The outcome had his one leg dangling against the outside glass panels, while the rest of him wrestled with his confusion as to why he wasn't making any progress. The attic had originally been designed to be a recreational sunroom. After seeing the unobscured night sky one night, Samantha decided to leave the window as it is. It was one of the smaller pleasures she enjoyed. "I see you're winning..."

"I think I'm stuck."

"Any reason why you think making a jump through is gonna be a good idea?"

"Look. This was a mistake. I'm so sorry I bothered you. I just think I should leave." It was funny because it was the first near sensical thing he had said the entire night. If she didn't know any better, she would have said that the effects of the drug were starting to wear off.

"Alright, why don't you come to sit down and let momma explain?"

"Momma?"

"Never mind. That sounded weird, even for me. Climb down and take a seat. C'mon. You can do it. There we go..."

True to form, he sported another dress shirt with the top button undone. In the subsequent events of the night, other buttons had followed, and the loose flap of fabric hooked on something on the window frame. His descent was going well until then before he found himself straining against the shirt being pulled backward. A tearing noise followed, making some of the other buttons pop as his body stretched the fabric beyond its limits.

She rushed toward him before he fell and injured himself, helping him pull his arms out of the sleeves to not only save what remained of the shirt but also to save her window. He barreled forward, falling over his own feet before stabilizing himself against a wall.

"Oh, man. Can you please make the room stop spinning?" he pleaded.

"This ain't a merry-go-round my friend. The only thing spinning is you. I'm afraid I don't have a button for that."

He turned around, leaning against the wall and trying to look at her with eyes that were swimming in his skull. Of course, it hadn't escaped her attention that he was half-naked as he stood in front of her. She would be remiss if she said she hadn't watched him for some time as his back muscles rippled beneath his olive skin while he was trying to orient himself while coming down. Standing there, looking all sheepish and confronted, her eyes had drunk in every bit of his toned physique like it was liquid fire. It left her parched for more, and her imagination couldn't help but undo the button of his jeans. *Keep it together Sam...keep it together*, she told herself. No wonder she went too far the first time. "Everything is so darn intense man..."

"Intense..." she mirrored, scoffing at the coincidence of the word.

"What? W—what's so funny?" He was becoming more alert. She wondered if he was gaining his memories back of everything he'd been up to until he got there.

"Nothing. I was just thinking about something I said a while back. So, uhm, the bathroom. I couldn't help but notice that you tried to use your blazer to cover it. Care to explain?"

"I, um—the bathroom," He put his hand to his forehead in an effort to concentrate. "Damn, how far gone am I?"

"Considering you wanted to take the quick way out from a slanted window, and the fact that you're losing your clothing around the house, I'd venture you've been pretty far down the rabbit hole." Looking down, she noticed his shoes were also gone. She didn't even know how to begin that conversation.

"The bathroom...yeah, uhm, aren't you self-aware in front of that big window? I mean, the neighbor could potentially—"

"Have a little show when I shower?" she finished for him. She didn't mind, to be honest. Her neighbor was hot. She was sure he didn't mind either. His girlfriend really didn't seem to mind, which left Sam with even more questions. Not that Sam cared about that either. "Why? Do I have something to be self-aware of?"

"N—no. You're..." he gulped. "You're beautiful! Really! It's just—ah..."

"Relax. I'm tormenting you. Look, you've had a little fun with the drug wizard's finest selection, but you seem to be climbing out of the kaleidoscope. You've also had a little bit to drink, so I have no idea how that may slow the process. We just need to get you on track. First things first..." she started, walking over to a pull-out drawer beneath her bed to whip out an oversized shirt, "put that on. You're distracting me."

He missed catching it as she flung it toward him. As he picked it up, it fell open. "This is a guy's shirt, like a large one. You wear this?" The look of post-trip confusion was almost adorable on his face. She forced down a laugh, trying to display some sympathy for his struggle.

"Men's shirts are the best sleepwear. It's like a mini nighty. Far more comfortable than anything in the women's aisle. I come home, take it all off, and just throw that bad boy on. It's cool and airy. Just my standard home wear."

"You just walk naked around the house? With all these windows open?" he asked with a hint of judgment.

"Watch it, buddy. That's a serious double-standard if ever there was one. From the amount of similar white shirts you have, I imagine you're one of those bare-chested gamers that play the night away...or you have an OnlyFans account that your buddies don't know of."

"OnlyFans? What the hell is that?" he asked, pulling the shirt over his head. It actually fit him perfectly.

"Damn, you sure are innocent, aren't you?"

"Isn't that why you're going to help me out," he countered.

What did he mean by that? His words were almost naughty, she thought to herself, but his expression was dead serious. *Could it be possible he's regaining some of his wit already?*

"You've got a smart mouth on you, you know. Even when you're not properly out of your tin can of illusions. At least I'm getting somewhere with you. Are you any closer to the 'real' reason you came to my house?" She sat on the edge of her bed, considering him with her arms folded.

He massaged his temple as if to clear away some of the fog on his mind. "You're not gonna let up are you?"

"Nope. I was perfectly on my way to settling in for a fabulous Friday evening." *Lies, of course. But he didn't need to know that.*

"Well...I mean, I told you didn't I? You had a friend who seemed to know you pretty well. I talked about you, he gave me your address."

"Oh yeah, that part I got. Me and Jimmy Valium will have a serious discussion about that."

"His surname is Valium?"

"He was the go-to college kid for depressants when people were way too pent up about studies. It was kind of a nickname he had. He's been dealing in some more potent stuff since then, but the name still has a ring to it. *Besides* the point though...*why* did you come?"

He took a deep breath to steady his thoughts, blinked a couple of times, and then answered. "Why does any guy get up to stupid stuff at impossible hours? It's because they have a guilty conscience, or because they've been thinking too hard about something."

So then which is it? Sam wondered. The way he said it nearly dispelled all animosity she had harbored toward him. He didn't show up at her house in the best shape, but she suspected there was far more to the story than she was actually seeing. "Are you...feeling any different?"

He seemed puzzled by his own thoughts for a moment as he considered the question. It was cute the way he squinted as if to concentrate. His furrowed brow made him look pensive and mysterious, and he had this quirk of pulling the corner of his mouth to the side which accentuated his strong jaw.

"Hot. Just...really hot and restless. Is that normal?"

It wasn't the answer she expected, but she couldn't say that she harbored any problems with it. "Totally," she lied.

Behave Samantha...behave.

Chapter 4:
Scaffolding

She leaned against the frame of the door, looking at the outstretched figure of a guy who she barely knew lying on her couch. Meredith seemed to have forgiven Gareth for his transgressions the previous night. She looked more than content to roll up into a little bread loaf on his chest. She casually spared a look Samantha's way.

"Bitch," Samantha mouthed, as she narrowed her eyes at her cat.

The entire situation felt very surreal to her. After a hectic work week that had barely allowed her to touch base with her personal life, she had arrived home feeling completely unsure of how to even settle in and acclimatize, much less being left alone. The next thing she knew, there was a man on her doorstep. The same man who had bred such fervent animosity inside of her after leaving her alone right after his string of advances. To top it all off, he was drunk and hallucinating. Now, the morning after, he was on her couch and she had no idea how to even start a conversation with him.

*Maybe breakfast. Food was always a great space filler for the company. If no one was talking, at least their mouths would be busy doing something. **If** someone were to talk, then doing so on a full stomach may be easier.*

She convinced herself that her idea was a good one while she walked over to the kitchen. The idea fell in on itself after opening the first empty cupboard.

She remembered that she hadn't done any shopping.

Even the bread tin was empty, and she seriously questioned the value of priorities if she couldn't even make a piece of toast.

As she looked around her pristine kitchen with all its empty promises of utility, her dejection was overcome by the saving grace of a strong Ugandan blend standing proudly on the shelf. She immediately got a brew going on her gas stove, the old Bialetti percolator doing a fine job to help her save face.

As it finished—dousing her in its strong, earthy aromas—she found herself steadily working up the courage to face the morning.

"God, please tell me you're making double."

Her head spun around in surprise, and she nearly spilled over the edge of the rim of one mug. "Jesus! You move way too quietly. I'd thought you'd be dragging your feet along you once you woke up."

He leaned against the kitchen entrance, his eyes barely open beneath his still-heavy lids. "I'm ashamed to say that I've had some practice with mornings like this." He rubbed at his eyes in a languid fashion and then tried to look at her through a squint.

"Seems like you want me to switch the morning off altogether," she responded. She handed him the steaming cup once the brew was made. Taking it was the only graceful gesture he was capable of. The rest of him seemed to be lagging two thoughts behind the rest.

"I'd really appreciate that," he said, trying to seem amused with a face that was still half-asleep.

She smirked, knowing that he could hardly see. "Drink up, Tarzan. You're not quite programmed for Saturday morning yet."

"Tarzan?" he asked, looking puzzled.

"The tree limb on the oak outside has seen better days. Your entrance last night was spectacular, but it had a price," she answered.

The uncertainty on his face persisted, even after he took a sip of coffee. He only seemed to process what she had meant much later. He drew his hand over his face as some of the memory came flooding back, and she found it funny how a face that looked like death could get so much color with a little embarrassment. "Oh my god. Last night was a spectacular shitshow wasn't it?"

"Well hey, I didn't see most of it. Next thing I knew you were inside and traipsing around while chasing after your imagination. I was just impressed you made a jump like that."

"You really did see me at my worst. I don't know how I'll redeem my image after that."

Samantha scoffed before pulling out a chair to sit at the kitchen table. "Listen, if we all worried about redemption, then we'd never get around to actually making the mistakes. Relax. I think the magic mushrooms were the dominant personality for most of your night."

"You said you knew Jimmy?"

"So well that I think your arrival here last night was no accident."

"Oh...yeah. I remember now. He gave me the address."

"Which brings me to the burning question I have for you. How did *that* conversation go down, that it brought you all the way to my doorstep?"

He took a deep breath in, rubbing the back of his head as he regarded her. "I think I might need breakfast for that."

"This is the most work I've had to do to get a single story out of someone," she said, as she took a giant sip from her mug.

***

"Say something," he prodded.

"I'm trying."

"Try harder, please," he jokingly pleaded, smiling as his mouth was half-filled with the flapjacks he had nearly decimated on his plate.

Her finger was playing on the rim of her glass, the orange juice untouched as she had listened to his account of the previous night in a mixture of surprise and amusement. "You expect me to believe that a stag party got so out of hand that you ended up on my front porch?"

He shrugged. "I've been to wilder stag parties."

"*Wilder* stag parties? Alright then. You'll have to walk me through this one. What windows of private property did those events have you climbing through?"

"Well, I think I ended up in a church once. The munchies had me eating the bread meant for the Sunday Communion."

She brought her hand to rest against her temple, staring at him from beneath a hooded brow. "Is this...just your default mode when you're asked to be a groomsman?"

His reaction was unexpected then. The smile he gave her in answer was solemn, almost as if a string of questions had been unleashed in his mind. "Nah, I'd say...call it bad choices, for lack of having better coping mechanisms."

She raised her head then, feeling how the concern was starting to play on her features. "Coping mechanisms?"

He nodded. "I've never really had bad ones, to be honest. I know that sounds rich, coming from a guy who showed up drunk and tranced at your home last night. But, if I'd known how to use them correctly, then I wouldn't be doing crazy shit like that."

"So then, what did you need to cope with?"

He twisted his mouth from side to side while he looked at his plate as if he was chewing on words that he desperately wanted to share but felt hesitant to. "Yeah. Let's not ruin breakfast with that. I'm sorry. Didn't mean to be a buzzkill."

Samantha narrowed her eyes at him, leaning forward on her elbows to bring her face closer in an expression that was playfully intimidating. "Listen, you may have killed my buzz once on that first night, but I'm a girl that makes the same kind of mistake only once."

"Sam, it's heavy. God, I think this counts as our first proper meeting. To lay that on you now—"

"*Proper* meeting? Ha. Now those are predictable. I prefer those candid and gritty kinds of meetings that give you the honest take of a person a lot sooner. Listen, buddy, if you're still hanging on to the first impressions stint, let me remind you: that moment walked out the door face first! Last night should be enough of a searing reminder," she laughed. "And besides, our eyes were already having sex that first night we grinded on the dancefloor. So just calm do— Wait. Are you *blushing*?"

"No. Why would I—"

"I can't believe it," she interjected. Sam sat back, folded her arms, and took his sheepish expression in with an amused smile. "Here I convinced myself you're such a player. Instead, you're just that textbook kind of nice guy with the surprising sensual quirk and a dash of awkwardness. All those looks and he doesn't know what to do with them."

He picked up his fork, grumbling as he pierced another piece of the syrup-drenched sin on his plate. "You know," he started, trying to be serious, "you can't just label a guy like that. We're a bit more complex."

"Oh, I have no doubts about that. Trust me, you're a Rubik's cube I've been trying to solve since you got cold feet that first night."

He stopped chewing for a moment, giving her a look that was somewhere between a smolder and a plea for some sympathy. It was such a disjointed expression. She couldn't help but find it sweet. "Yeah, about that. I should probably say I'm sorry..."

Sam still kept up a half-smile, acknowledging the sincerity. The busy week had all but diminished her irritation of that night, even though she was left thinking about him sometimes. "What *did* happen to you?"

He sighed while chewing, finding a place to start his explanation. "It comes back to the stuff I was coping with. Remember that phone call?"

"It's seared into memory," she taunted, winking at him.

He lightened up, smiling as he ate, before continuing. "Well, I got a call from the building manager saying that a woman had gone up to my studio apartment. She claimed to be Mrs. Wakeford, and she was allowed in by security."

"What the—Whoa, whoa, whoa. Hold on. First of all, why would security just allow someone in the building on a mere claim? Second, why would a chick rock up and claim to be your wife?"

He sat back then as if preparing for a verbal barrage. *Oh, boy. Here it comes. A guy with a history. Way to pick them, Sam.*

"I can answer both those questions at the same time. She was my wife once."

Sam exhaled, resting her head on her hand as if she felt tired of the story already—even though she was interested. She had heard it all while she had dated through the years, even if she was still in her twenties. "Ok. Go on. I'm listening. An ex, huh?"

"One with many hang-ups. Although, it's unfair for me to say so. Abby has always had a couple of problems."

"Still, why did the guard let her in? If you're divorced, then—"

"It was a misunderstanding. Estaban, the guard, was on night watch. Pure coincidence would have it that he only met Abby once, and never had a run-in with her again after that. Suffice it to say, he didn't have any idea we weren't together anymore. She is a pathological liar though, so she charmed her way inside."

"Damn. That's bad luck."

He nodded. "When I got the call, I had to rush home. My last confrontation with Abby was anything but friendly. Knowing how unstable she is, I was afraid she would unearth some work files I've been keeping under lock and key."

"You know people use cloud storage today, right?"

"Not for this. Even cloud storage is unsafe if hacked. Sometimes, the older methods are best. Regardless, she could have done some real damage if she decided to."

"So why is she such a walking hazard?"

"A couple of years ago, she started manifesting signs of early-onset bipolar disorder. I didn't understand what was happening, but her periods of mania were hectic enough to deal with. We saw many specialists and gained her access to the best treatment. At a time, things did look better. Even though it was brief. But sometimes without me knowing, she stopped her medication. She incurred a hell of a lot of financial losses on my behalf, not to mention other damage she caused. It drove a wedge between us, and I had to let her go. I didn't leave her to fend for herself, I tried to get her help so that she could get her life back on track. But, she disappeared, and even her family hindered me from trying to contact her."

"Wow. I—I don't know what to say. It's—almost kind of creepy."

"I'm not one to scare easily," Gareth started, speaking softly, "but Abby, at her worst, *was* scary. Nearly uncontrollable. When she drifted back into my life like some phantom a week ago, it really set me on edge."

"Is she...back for good then?"

"No. But, she's here. She's around. That's enough to unsettle me. She knows where I live. And despite everything she has to deal with on a mental health level, she is smart and resourceful. The instability of her emotions is being channeled through her spite. That makes her completely unpredictable. I've implemented additional security measures now, and since then made it public that I'm divorced. But, I'm sleeping with one eye open at night. And even her family has started to hound me. They...just have the proclivity to make things extra difficult."

Samantha felt like crap for even getting upset all those nights ago. She may not have known the full scope of Gareth's situation, but she only began to imagine the difficulties he'd been saddled up with. "How—how long were you married?"

"About five years."

"Whoa, you must have been in your early 20s?"

"We both were. High school sweethearts. In fact, her family had almost adopted me in some way after the death of my own parents."

"My condolences."

He brushed it off. "It happened long ago. Anyway. My attachment to her wasn't a direct result of their help and generosity. We—Nevermind. You really don't want to hear about that."

"No, no. Please. Go ahead," she prodded, lightly brushing his forearm with the tips of her fingers. Even in light of the slightly dour nature of their conversation, the touch felt electric. "I want to hear."

He smiled, silently reflecting the same emotion. "We were immediately drawn to one another. She was my first real crush. I'd dated many girls before we ever became a thing, but it was the first time a physical, mental, and emotional attraction aligned for me in that way. It took us such a long time to act on it, even after we lived in the same house. I mean, it's confusing, don't you think? Liking the girl of the family you're being assimilated into. She was supposed to feel like my sister. Perhaps her parents knew. They never did file for adoption, instead, finding some other way to maintain legal guardianship without me having to assume the family name. I dated other girls while I lived with them. But after high school, there was only her. And we finally gave it a shot, For those first few years—like any story pertaining to one's first love—it was almost idyllic. God, it's almost surreal to think how soon everything started to change after that..."

"I can understand that."

He looked up then, almost as if realizing that she was still listening. "I don't feel that way about her anymore! Obviously. We've been divorced for a year now, and things had gone south long before that. I—"

"Hey, hey. Relax, alright. There's no shame in acknowledging how you once felt about someone. That is denying a crucial part of who you once were. I think you really loved her and tried to be supportive. But there were obviously situational factors that wrestled it all from your control."

"Hmph. Sometimes, I have to tell you, I wondered if I could do more. But I didn't understand it then, as I do now." Gareth had his eyes cast down in some infinity of his memory, and she wondered how much he had suppressed his efforts to be a buffer to everyone but himself. "I wish her well, still. Even after all the damage she had done. Maybe I love her in a way too. But it's a love of a vibrancy that she once had. Now, believe it or not, fear is the overriding emotion. I just don't know what she'll do next."

Sam cocked her head slightly to the side. "You're a psychedelic stag party survivor who drives over the curb, swings from trees, finds a girl he met once or twice, and licks cats while stuck in his tin can of hallucinations. And you're afraid of her?" She smiled at him knowingly.

He chuckled, and it appeared her attempt to lighten the mood had worked. "Yeah, well... finding courage from recreational substances doesn't seem like the royal road to healing."

"I second that. But hey, at least the stories do."

He seemed to ease up then, his appetite renewed as he wolfed down the last of his breakfast. The Country Road Deli was one of the oddest installments to the Hampton dining experience. Amid a vast collection of venues that catered to finer cuisine or niche markets, the deli seemed like such an average spot for food that didn't aim to be anything beyond what it was—a hearty meal. It made the spot a rather wholesome experience among all the pretension in the area and was envied for its location, built on the banks of the body of water separating Southampton and Bridgehampton. It was another exquisite Saturday, all the more so because the middle-class appeal of the place attracted real people with an authentic diversity. Perhaps they were all the Hampton rejects—forced into the life while never wanting it. She felt right at home.

"Speaking of stories," he started again, "what is the story behind the scowl of rejection you gave me the other day—at the East Hampton Brunch Club."

She didn't immediately catch his meaning, but then felt the sour twinge in her mood as she recalled the moment he was referring to. "Oh, I'm sure you know exactly what the story behind that look was. Better question, what the hell were you even doing there?"

He finished chewing before he answered. "So...this family I was sort of adopted into is part of the club."

"Abby's parents are one of the Hampton dynasties?"

"Mm-hm. They have been for a while. When I reached my 16th birthday, they started taking me along. It's always been an opulent waste of time, money, and energy in my opinion."

"My parents organize those events," Samantha remarked.

Gareth nearly choked on his coffee, grabbing at a napkin to no doubt catch the foot falling out of his mouth. "I'm sorry," he coughed, "I didn't mean to—"

"Oh no, please! I'm not disagreeing with you. Imagine what I must think after attending events like that for years. It's like they're holding on to the glory of a bygone era. One day, the pressed collar shirt look and cocktail dress fantasy will fade in the preference of branded active sportswear—judging by today's fashion standards. There are more laid back ways to display exclusivity."

"And to network—which is why I was there. Well, *actually*, I was there to stroke the egos of a few retired Harvard University Professors whom we wish to reel in for fellowship ties to Fordham University. I work in the Philosophy Department there. I received a tip-off that they had crawled out from under a rock to finally attend a social event. Despite what happened the previous night, I had to take a chance."

"And instead you were meant with the fiery scorn of a woman," she teased.

"Actually, I happened to talk to them before I bumped into you." He breathed a sigh of relief. "Jesus, I'm glad it happened in that order. I was tongue-tied after walking into you there. I wouldn't have been able to get a word out."

She raised an eyebrow at him. "Felt intimidated, did you?"

"Uh, yeah. You're a formidable woman, Claremont—" He experienced a facepalm moment. "Claremont...of course! I should have made the connection."

"You couldn't have known. It's ok. The less you associate me with the 'lion's pride,' the better. I'm curious how you still attend those meetings though. I mean, listen, you can totally fit in as the new-age legacy with your faux hawk style and clean-cut look, but the club usually has a rotating VIP list."

"I still receive invites every time, purely by the association I had to the Bianchis."

A chill went down Samantha's spine. *It couldn't be.* She must have misheard that. "The who?"

"The Bianchis. You must know them. Well, their family is pretty extensive, I'll give you that. But nearly all of them are known to some degree or another. Abby was the daughter of Vincenzo Bianchi, the Italian small business magnate."

She knew Vincenzo. She also knew the rest of his family quite extensively, more than a few who made bed with questionable affairs. She fought down her initial reaction lest it displayed on her face. His latest confession had taken her aback, but she couldn't allow it to define her interaction with Gareth. Her history with the family was muddled and she just hoped that any enduring memory of her would have faded with time.

"I don't really see them much anymore. Only by accident. It's strange that Manhattan still can feel so small despite being so large."

"You're telling me…"

"Hey, uhm, are you going to eat that?"

She looked at where he was pointing, realizing that her breakfast had remained virtually untouched. "Uh, no. No, I think I—I think I lost my appetite," she pushed the plate his way, seeing the hunger in his eye.

"Thanks. Man, I'm famished." He dug in almost immediately, and perhaps she would have been more stunned by his ravenous appetite if she'd been more present. But the revelation of his social ties had given her pause. Even her hands were slightly shaky, and she steadied them against the cup of coffee the waitress had brought.

"So," he said, between another mouthful. "What are you up to today?"

"Hmm?" she responded, her head whipping up as if waking from a dream. "Oh, uhm. Well, I need to go see a friend of mine at an art exhibit tonight.

"That's cool. You're an artist then?"

"Of sorts. I fell in love with photography. We sort of have a collaborative relationship with the kinds of exhibits we choose to form part of. His niche is performance art and this is what these exhibits are all about. I hooked him up with some of the models that I work with as part of my main hustle, and in turn, he allows me to photograph them for my purposes once he's transformed them. So, I usually also give him a couple of photos to use as part of his portfolio. Some of the more intricate shots I use as part of mine."

"I love exhibits…"

Don't do it, Samantha. "You can totally come." *Dammit.* "I'm sure he'd appreciate looking at you as much as he looks at his 'art.' Just don't let him draw you in."

"Ha! What kind of exhibit is this in any way?"

"The theme is Celestial Bodies."

"Wasn't that the theme of the Met Gala once?"

"Uhm…well yes. But the Met never did a nude version."

Chapter 5:
Instructional Play

Samantha didn't envision herself spending the entire day with Gareth. At most, she'd convinced herself that he'd hightail it out of her house the minute she interrogated him. But—she had to remind herself—a 28-year-old probably didn't suffer the emotional inflexibility of a pre-teen. Gareth was capable of owning up to his mistakes, and even to be seen at his worst.

And she had seen worse, much worse, the more she thought about it. She had witnessed other men befriend alien substances for a night with some spectacular results. When a man cried it was never pretty. When a man compounded all his emotions into personal philosophies about the state and purpose of meaning, even less so. Somehow, Gareth had survived his psychedelia with a kind of slick nobility, doing some impressive things such as driving and jumping onto the second floor of a building. Not to mention the moment he then proceeded to lose his clothes in some clumsy striptease that soon made Samantha forget all the insanity.

Not only did he stay, but he explained it all, sharing more of his backstory than she thought even Viola or Blanche may have shared in all their years of friendship. What had originally been the suave and sexy philanderer in her mind turned out to be just another guy with a set of human vulnerabilities. He was still hot though, and much of him was still a mystery. Only now, he somehow no longer seemed to be beyond her comprehension, and it invited a more sincere side of herself to the table.

Before breakfast, they returned the car he had parked so close to her front door—a car that turned out to belong to the groom-to-be from the wild bachelor's party the night before. After charging his phone, a string of missed calls prompted him to some action. There was a drop-off and then an exchange, in which he got his own car back. The remaining retinue of the stag party was there. Samantha quite enjoyed seeing Jimmy squirming back into a corner as he spotted her. He clearly had a few unresolved issues to reflect on.

Afterward, Gareth coaxed her to tag along to his place. After all, he had reasoned, it was much closer to the David Zwirner Gallery, where the performance art exhibit was set to take place. His logic was sound, she had to reluctantly admit to herself. He lived on the edge of Queens, in a studio apartment that overlooked the East River. For her, it would have been quite the drive, even if she was used to it. Her home was in Babylon, about 30 miles from the westernmost tip of the city. So she succumbed and packed a vanity case and her attire for the evening's event. With further encouragement, she packed an overnight bag as well, on condition that he'd drop her off at a friend's afterward.

She wasn't sure why she was being so agreeable with a man whom she had known for such a short time. Regardless, she tagged along, feeling compelled for some unknown reason to spend more time with him. Throughout the drive, however, the details of his past started tugging at her mind Gareth didn't know about her reservations and the way she couldn't help but wonder whether she was playing with fire. She decided to push her concerns to the side for the time being.

On many levels, she was also still piecing him together. He was masculine, yet metrosexual; his demeanor was smooth, yet slapstick; he was clever, yet casual. She had never kept company with academics as far as she recalled. Somehow, he had become an entirely new species all in himself. *What did a guy with a Ph.D. in philosophy even find appealing? How would he decorate his house?* Samantha didn't know what to expect as she walked into his home.

The mystery was soon broken. Walking into his place, she was reminded of the office of a rich Southern state tycoon; right before it morphed into something that emulated a hipster jazz lounge. It created an ambiance that seemed adorned with the hypermasculine scent of power and cedarwood, while the smell of coffee wafted through the air. His aesthetic was profiled by leather and wood, lending the space a rustic feel that seemed juxtaposed with the gleaming city beyond. Nearly every empty space was filled with a houseplant—all of them alive, which she considered a miracle. His taste in art was eclectic, including a multitude of mediums and styles that he supplemented from what must have been a life of extensive travel. Perhaps the only part that correlated with her schema of his place was the space that acted as his study, which was a desk pushed against the far side window overlooking the city, flanked by massive bookshelves groaning with the amount of knowledge stacked upon them. It was a writer's space, and she could almost see him sitting there while absorbed by his midnight musings with a typewriter, pounding away under the watchful glow of a desk lamp and the sleepless city.

"What?" he asked, noticing as she looked around while walking in.

"Oh, nothing."

"You look...scrupulous. Almost judgmental."

"Of course I do. It's what gives me my charm."

"So hit me with that charming opinion of yours," he prodded.

"They say you can really judge a man by his sense of decor."

"*They* say that? Who's *they*?"

"My mother," she answered coyly.

"Of course. Right, right," he played along, "and what did she teach you to do with those judgments?"

"To reserve them. To keep them as ammunition. There's no better way to shoot down a man's pride than through the right choice of words," she winked at him. "Luckily, I doubt any of that will be necessary. You don't need to bite the bullet. I think your place has...personality."

He scoffed. "Was that your first summary of me back in the club all those nights ago?"

"Maybe," she teased. "So, where can I change? We need to be there in an hour."

"The bathroom's in that alcove to the side," he pointed.

"Thanks." She swung her garment bag over her shoulder, flashed him a smile, and strutted in the direction he pointed through the space that acted as his bedroom.

The bathroom was an eclectic fixture in itself, fusing sleek modernism and Grecian romanticism. It was the type of space that must have seen many a woman seduced, and have her see the surrender to carnal pleasures in the full-length mirror on the opposite wall. Staring at herself, Samantha could not help but allow her thoughts to dwell. She imagined how she would stand there fully undressed, and see strong hands slipping over her figure from behind as the tantric dance began. The thought dispersed as she heard wardrobe doors being opened, realizing that Gareth was in the room just beyond. The door to the bathroom was ajar, but she was still hidden from view.

She slipped out of her casual wear, and into the midnight blue number she had brought for the occasion. The thigh-length dress hugged her bodice, and modestly covered her bust. From there, a translucent slip of fabric reached up to a low-reaching lace collar, leaving only the neck, arms, and legs exposed. She paired it off with black strap-heeled sandals and silver dangle earrings.

"Hey...what did you say the dress code for this gig was?"

"Smart casual. One of those crisp white shirts you wore the other night should work fine. If you can find one that isn't torn," she playfully hinted.

"I was thinking...*this*. What do you think?"

"Coming. Give me one sec," she said, whilst putting on the last bit of jewelry, "and... done." She walked into the bedroom. "Okay, so show me w—"

She stopped short, watching as Gareth stood half-naked in front of his bed, wearing nothing but his briefs. The late afternoon light wrapped around his muscular frame as he held a shirt in each hand. It was as though he was made of liquid metal, with the light dancing over his tight olive skin. He was exquisite, every ounce of him, and her eyes drank every detail in heavily before he noticed her staring and held up the shirts in front of himself to show her. "Ah, there you are. So, which one pops more?"

"Uhm...on second thought, the black would really suit you better."

He let the shirts drop and she caught her breath as she got another glimpse before he smiled and fitted on her choice. "You know, it's a bit ironic that we're getting dressed for an event that celebrates nudity."

"You're telling me," she said. *I'd celebrate it right here.* "Wait, don't do up the buttons all the way."

"Huh?" he said, as his fingers fumbled with the button at the chest.

"You want to open the imagination, not close it. We're headed to an art exhibit after all. Besides, it's best to distract Julio before he bellows out odes to the naked form." *And I wouldn't mind a distraction myself.*

***

Slow music pulsed through the gallery and weaved itself among the hiss of a hundred whispers. The exhibit was another filthy extravagance, non-surprisingly attended by some of the most beautiful people Samantha had ever seen together in a single room. Naturally, the guest list did not fall short of reflecting Julio's pervy preferences. What made it stand out from similar occasions was that they were surrounded by people whose looks didn't depend on cosmetics or lavish accessories. Instead, they were all apex specimens by genetics.

Samantha had been around such collectives before but still found it alien. She could tell Gareth was enthralled, although she believed his interests were more inquisitive than lusting.

She had to force down a laugh as he leaned in to make a special study of one of a couple of models that had been painted to resemble crashing waves. The effect of their fluid motions was mesmerizing, mimicking that of a sea in motion. Their bodies intertwined gracefully, and yet with such force that it was a wonder that the paint didn't shift. Gareth was awestruck as the nude forms of the two men flowed on that pedestal, and she caught at least one of them smiling at how much they had snared their onlooker.

"Better close your mouth buddy, or you'll catch a mouth full of water," she said as she came up to his side.

He jumped ever so slightly. "Huh? Oh, sorry! God, I'm just so intrigued by all this. You know, my entire life has been spent deciphering liberalist philosophies that only talk of unshackling the body and mind to obtain its ultimate freedoms. And here you have an entire event celebrating it."

"Welcome to my world," she cooed.

"There she is! The one that got away."

The voice came from their back, thickly accented, and Samantha turned to see Julio Hernandez glide toward her with outstretched arms. For the elaborate gesture, his embrace was never anything more than the flutter of a butterfly's wings as he touched you on the back. What assailed you instead was the heady perfumes he wore which she could only describe as a fragrant bouquet dropped in the desert. His curly head of hair was swept back to frame his sharp face, adorned with the exquisite mustache.

"It's good to see you, Jules. This is my—well, I brought some company along. This is Gareth."

"Well, well. *¡Un hombre tan guapo!* What a creature you've brought along. Is he for the exhibit?" he excitedly asked as he undressed Gareth with his eyes.

"Only to appreciate the art I'm afraid," she reproved with a smile.

He sighed. "Tsk tsk. So you dangle another potential in front of me that I cannot proudly transform for the world. This is a shame."

"And how would you paint me, Julio?" Gareth chimed in, quite unexpectedly.

Samantha was gobsmacked by his playful response, and so was Julio. He looked stunned for a moment before something akin to amusement and mischief coalesced into an expression of pure glee. "Ha! Well now. Not just a handsome face, but a handsome mind. I'd paint you with the ink I never used in writing to lovers that are now long gone...and your body will be the vessel of all my secrets."

"My, my... You're a lucky man. He's never offered *me* that before."

"Ah, *pero mi amor.* But I offer you all this!" he said, placing a hand on her shoulder while he gestured to the entire gallery with a wide sweep of his arm. "We will allow the beautiful people to get lost in Wonderland for half an hour more before I start making speeches and we move to the courtyard. You are welcome to my creations then!" Before more could be said, he pranced off to dote on yet another one of the guests.

"You're the one that got away huh? If even gay men tell you that, then you must be more of a heartbreaker than I thought," Gareth said.

"Oh, he is completely pansexual. Julio has made a number of advances. He's also wanted to make me one of his canvases for years. But I've declined him many times."

"Why? I think that's quite flattering."

The question drew more somberness from her than she intended, as a flicker of the past alighted on her mind. "Many men are flattering. It isn't all with good intentions."

"Hey...uhm. It was meant as a compliment. I just think you're gorgeous, that's all."

She snapped out of her mood and offered him a smile. "Well, aren't you just full of interesting things to say?" she winked at him. "So, why don't you go gawk at more installations. I want to get a head start on some of the models that don't have a cluster of spectators in front of them."

"Sure! You sure you don't need any help?"

"Nope. The lighting and everything else is perfect, which negates the need for hefty equipment. I'm just going to be swerving around with my camera. You enjoy it. I'll meet up with you after. Oh, but Gareth..."

"Yeah?"

"Try not to touch the exhibit," she winked at him before disappearing among the guests.

***

Merriment replaced the almost subdued appreciation that dominated the gallery at the start. The speeches had been made, the gratitude extended—with little humility to spare—and all the guests had mingled long enough to have found their company for the evening.

Surprisingly, she found Gareth socializing as well, talking to a group of women that could have been Amazonian in some mythic accounts. The moment he spotted her, he smiled and excused herself, walking to meet her halfway.

"So? How'd it go? Did you get what you needed?"

"Mm-hm," she affirmed, holding up the camera for emphasis. "There's another exhibit that I'll be a part of in the Hamptons in about three weeks' time. I'll be editing some of these as the final additions to my entry."

"That's great!" he said, looking far more excited than she had anticipated.

"Oh my god. What did you do?"

"What do you mean?" he asked, faking innocence.

"You're way too wound up not to be up to something..."

"Well," he said, taking her by the hand, "I think I'm growing progressively worse at spinning stories, so let me just show you." He started walking, pulling her gently along.

"Where are we going?" she asked while he dragged her through the other people in attendance to a doorway leading into a closed-off section of the gallery. "I don't think it's—" she started, before the handle twisted and he pushed the door open by a crack to allow them to slip through.

Samantha expected to walk into pitch darkness, but a soft illumination from the dimmed lighting lined the corridors. He took her hand again, taking them both down a passageway that eventually allowed them to reach a flight of stairs.

"Ready for a climb?" he asked mischievously.

"Hold on," she answered, removing her strap-on heels before ascending the flights with him. "We're not really supposed to do this you know."

"Correction. Your friend came up to me a few minutes before he addressed his guests. He said that if I placed value on the company I keep, then I'd better make more of an effort to woo you. He happened to know a place."

"Oh, really? I think Julio likes creating all kinds of scenarios. He's also fairly good at finding a place for them. You shouldn't believe everything the man says."

"I figured I'd take my chances with this one," he answered, as they reached the top. "He gave me this!" He removed a key from his pocket and proceeded to unlock the door that barred their way.

"This leads to the roof..." she noted.

"Damn straight."

"But what's so special about—" she was shut down as the door opened into a lavish rooftop garden. "Whoa..." she just barely got out.

"I know, right!" he said, closing the door behind them. "He said he'd created Eden. I didn't know what he meant until much later."

"All of this...is new," she said in awe. Looking around, one could nearly forget that you were on a roof in the first place. Julio had clearly been busier than he'd let on. She didn't know how he'd even gotten the permission, but then again, Julio was one of the most persuasive people she had ever come across.

A stone walkway led to a micro courtyard splitting off into three other directions ending on the edges of the roof. Surrounding it, he had planted rows upon rows of flowers and other greenery that both merged and complemented statues and rock formations, while solar lamps were expertly placed to create a secluded little fantasy under the night sky. Wispy tendrils drifted up from mist-making water features. And looking at it all, she wondered if anyone at all had ever seen it.

"Did he...switch all this on for us? The lights, the display?"

"Seems like it. It's beautiful isn't it?"

Samantha walked to the center and looked up. It was impossible to see the stars in the city. New York would always be its own celestial feature. But dominating the clear sky, she did see the moon. It was a sickle tonight. One of her most mundane and yet most beautiful memories, was when her mother had told her that a little man sat on that sickle to watch the world below. The romanticism soon faded when she saw her first *DreamWorks* movie, realizing that her mother may have described nothing more than the logo. She should have known it was too good to be true. Her mother was never one for entertaining idle childhood fantasies.

But if there had been someone watching from that sickle, she wondered what he would have seen as he looked down on that garden. Julio had also teased he wanted to surrender his body in wild lust and abandon in a wilderness, but one that he himself created. She couldn't help but wonder whether this entire garden had not been thrown together for the entertainment of some tasty and illicit affairs.

"Hey, check this out," he called out from the enclosure of small trees to her side. He was only barely visible in the muted glow of lamps scattered throughout the garden. It cast deep shadows within the hollows of his cheeks and the angular edges of his strong neck and jaw, and he looked every bit like the seductive nighttime prowler you only ever read about in dark fantasies.

There was an outdoor lounge chair made for two, fortified at the base and without any legs. It was decked out with soft patio cushions hidden among the foliage. It gave them an unobstructed view of the city and when laying down, the entire sky opened up above them.

Gareth stretched himself out on the seat, casting that marvelous face of his upward. "I think your Julio had some interesting intentions with this, don't you think? It's...romantic, even if in a clandestine way."

"A hidden lover's corner in the secret garden. I never thought of you as the sort."

"You didn't? Damn." He closed his eyes, with an elated smile on his face, folding his arms behind his head. "I've had the best sex of my life outside."

The confession took her aback so much that she'd spurted out a laugh.

He opened up one eye to look at her then. "What?" he asked sheepishly.

"I just—*ahem*. I just didn't expect that."

"Hmm. I'd love to climb into that head of yours," he mused. "You know, to get a peek at some of these expectations."

She looked back up to the sky just as the wind rustled her hair, thinking of his comment. "I'm always wary of expectations. There's too much self-ridden guilt and self-flagellation in that recipe. It leaves a bad taste in one's mouth."

"You know, you would have made a great contemporary philosopher. You have that profound, yet candid way about you."

"Really. Does it get you hard?"

"Ha!" he exclaimed. "I'm a sapiosexual, though and through. At least, that's what I've told myself. Until I realized that I'm nothing more than a base creature that gets aroused by a beautiful woman. So, you need to redeem me."

"*I* need to redeem *you*?" she responded.

"Yeah. Here you are, this wild, incandescent thing that caught my eye from the first second I laid eyes upon you. Tonight you remind me of that...that first time. I've fallen for beautiful women before. But I want my *mind* to be snared to your wiles as much as by your beauty."

"You make me sound dangerous..."

"Are you?"

"Terribly. I told you once before. But, your concerns are unnecessary. I think you're safe."

"Am I now?"

"Mm-hm. Asking questions like that can only warrant that I've meddled with your mind a bit. It's how I snared many men after all."

"Ha! Then I'm glad to be part of the club." He was still staring at the sky, and whatever uncertainty had clung to him before had all but melted away.

"Well, I think it's time we get out of here."

"Sure, sure. In a few minutes."

"Nope! Sorry. C'mon, before anyone forgets that we're even up here," she heaved, taking him by the hand to pull him to his feet. Reluctantly he cooperated and allowed himself to be dragged up.

Whether by some awkward motion or a misstep, both she and Gareth stumbled and fell back onto the cushions. She was lying with him beside her, uncertain how she got there. She sighed. "Ok. I'll give you another five minutes to chew on your thoughts. You clearly need it."

He turned toward her then, reclining on his elbow as he lay on his side. He was looking at her, while a smirk played at the corner of his mouth. "How would you know what I need? Hmm?" he taunted.

"Ah. There it is. I see you have that gleam in your eye."

"What gleam?" he asked, playing at innocence.

"The gleam of invincibility. Young, creatively inspired, sexually charged, and with testosterone coursing through your body. I bet you feel you can take over the world now."

"I feel I could do a couple of things right now, but we have a party to get back to. Don't we?" His eyes were wild and dark as he looked at her, drowning her with both it and his words.

Get a grip, Sam, she reprimanded herself.

"Guess you need to help me up then, otherwise I might never leave."

He smiled and placed a hand at her back. The other took her own hand, drawing her toward him. Following the flow of movement, she motioned to bring her feet beneath her to stand, but his own body blocked her.

She was close to him then, her chest pressed against his. His hold was firm as he cradled her. He did nothing for a few seconds, neither of them did. They merely allowed nerve endings to fire as their bodies pressed together. One of his hands moved up her back, gently coming to rest on the back of her neck.

His fingertips were electric against her skin. Soon, they disappeared in the long strands of her hair. He was bringing his hand up to lift her head, and she could already feel his warm breath dancing on her mouth—right before he parted it with his own. Her surrender to him was so absolute, so effortless, that she didn't waste energy to overthink the moment as it happened. At first, it was gentle, then it turned into a crush of his lips against hers. Their kisses became harder, then faster.

His hold on her was solid, and she pulled him closer to her as her legs wrapped around his lower half. It dragged him onto her, and they both sank into the soft pillowing while his kisses continued to flutter down her jaw and into her neck. She writhed in ecstasy. It was her soft spot. And he wreaked havoc on her mind as his mouth pressed against her hungrily.

Her hand shot out and dove beneath his clothes, feeling his feverish skin as her hand grazed up his side. He stopped then, and he slowly came up to loom over her before he removed his shirt. He was more beautiful to her then than he had ever been. In the sparse light that shone in that place, every muscle of his was accentuated more starkly. They rippled beneath tight skin, between heavy breaths, containing the smoldering fire that she could only see in his eyes.

Lowering himself down, he lifted her again to meet him. Their lips embraced like old lovers as soon as they touched. At her back, his hand had taken hold of the buttons to her dress, slowly starting to slide it off until he pulled it down her body in one swift motion.

He laid her down then, and his fingers grazed gently across the skin of her shoulders, down her arms, until they were level with her waist.

"You're perfect," he breathed, right before his hand traveled slowly up her middle. He was straddling her, keeping her locked in place as he explored every inch of her skin. He took his time, and she could feel her own pulse-quickening in anticipation of the beast that would awaken inside of him. She had been alive so many times, caught in the throes and adulation from a hundred lovers. Yet, she could never quite recall ever wanting someone as badly as she wanted him.

He was doing everything right, every touch landing expertly. But as she felt him swollen against her upper thigh, she wanted him to break all the rules. She wanted him to take her, rough and undisciplined, until she wouldn't know her name many hours later.

Pieces of clothing started to disappear after every revolution he made up and down her body. Between his hands and his lips, there were parts of her that never felt so constrained, and then so freed, until he removed each fabric to let her bask naked in front of him.

The most excruciating part was watching him unbutton his pants. They couldn't come off fast enough. The mysteries her imagination had conjured had made her more wanting than she wished to admit. But at that moment, she didn't care how desperate and needy it seemed. She wanted her way.

That's when she decided to take it.

The control shifted in an instant when nothing separated them. She rolled him on his back, pinning him beneath her thighs, and guided him into her.

They lost track of time...

Chapter 6:
Cautious Fun

"About fucking time! Where have you been?" Blanche confronted Samantha as she found her in one of the sections of the Blue Room Gallery close to Sea Harbor. It was the night of her exhibit. It was packed, to Samantha's disappointment—which was a strange feeling considering the work she put into it. Suddenly, she didn't feel all that hyped to be around some of the most esteemed artistic bodies of Long Island. There's only one body that she wanted.

"We...got occupied."

Blanche's eyes went wide. "You *brought* him? Where is he?" She looked appalled as she searched the gallery.

"He went to get us some drinks. Relax. Jesus. Why are you so wound up?"

Blanche looked back at her with accusation in her eye. "You didn't read my text, did you?"

"Clearly not. Otherwise, I might know what has you so high strung."

Blanche grabbed Samantha by the arm, dragging her around the corner of a wall to give them some privacy. "I was messaging to tell you not to bring your new toy because a complication arose about an hour ago.”

“A complication? You make it sound like we intended to meet on some covert operation.”

“When it concerns Emilio, everything is secret. That’s what we agreed! It’s your ex. He’s here,” Blanche said with urgency. “And trust me, he’s not going to be happy when he sees you have a plaything at your side.”

***

Emilio Bianchi had a dominating presence when he stood in a room. Part of it was credited to his height and muscular build. Not that it was definitive. Men like that weren't in short supply. Rather, he moved that body differently from other men. It seemed to Sam more like a panther coiling its muscles during a hunt. It lent him primal energy that he exuded wherever he went and left a glint of hunger in his eyes. And when you looked into them, you saw something wild, intelligent, and incredibly dangerous.

In fact, Samantha's thoughts were always drawn to that last description when she remembered something about him. Once upon a time, when innocence still marked her decisions, she was more susceptible to its charm. Danger seemed thrilling, if only for its unpredictability. But she knew better now.

The last thing she expected tonight was to be faced with such flashbacks. But with him standing right there, she could not hold back the flow of memory.

"Blanche, what the hell is he doing here?" Sam asked, her voice tenser than she wanted to acknowledge.

"You realize I'm the last person that would know that, right? I nearly let my glass fall when he came prowling in."

Prowling was a good word to describe the way he snuck through the crowd. He moved with intent. Lethal and graceful. He was turning more than one head as he walked past. Nearly every woman, and more than a few of the men, were gawking at this phenomenon that had stepped into the exhibit. Perhaps that was what gave him his edge—he owned the room the moment he entered.

Charisma and that kind of power ultimately draw attention. For others, like herself, it inspires blind belief and commitment to their ideals. Or at least, it did once. Since then, she had become increasingly better at refusing the things that didn't suit her. Emilio became the first man she ever refused.

He didn't like that.

"Look, maybe we can slip you out a different exit. The venue is filled with people. He might miss y–"

"He won't. Watch closely. He isn't just idling around in an attempt to mingle. Yes, he's playing it cool, but he's looking for someone. I know that look. It took me years to figure it out."

"Damn. You think he's looking for you?" Blanche's voice was a mixture of both nerves and excitement. Supportive as she was, she was a sucker for some drama.

"It's the only thing that ever brought him to this part of the world. I've invited him to a couple of these exhibitions. He never came. But he always asked about them afterward." *Right before he strung me along in his next big venture.* Emilio always listened, he listened not only to understand, but to leverage. He had always been interested in what she did. But he would always make sure that it didn't infringe on what *he* was doing.

"You don't have to stay, Sam. Whether he sees you or not, you can easily walk away."

For a second, that was exactly what she wanted to do. It was the simplest thing, to just leave old problems behind and avoid a complication. But there was a reason why Emilio had doted on her all those years ago when he could have any other woman. Samantha was stubborn, strong-willed, and equally as defensive of her wants. It was another one of those Claremont quirks.

"Bullshit," she responded. "Why should I? This is my exhibition as much as any other photographer present. I've worked hard to be here. Tonight, he's in *my* territory."

"Alright. Slow down 'lion pride.' I get you. But you're forgetting that you won't be squared off against him alone. You have another man at your side. That gives Emilio a distinct advantage once he picks up on that because he'll be fueled by jealousy. *If* he's here to find you, then he'll definitely try to make it uncomfortable. "

She was right, even though Sam was reluctant to admit it. Gareth was nowhere to be seen, and her eyes were searching across groups of people huddled in front of the different portraits.

"I need to find Gareth."

"What are you going to tell him?"

"I have no idea. But I need the chess pieces in front of me before I can play the game." She had to apply some tactics. Alone, she could handle Emilio. With Gareth to consider, her need to protect him might make her less strategic.

"What do you need me to do?"

"Look for him as well. If you find him first, I need you to keep him occupied in a different section of the exhibition. Tell him that I'll be joining shortly."

"And if you find him first?"

"Then let's hope I can outrun one of the infamous Italian stallions." She surveyed the crowd again, this time looking for Emilio. To her dismay, he too had vanished. "Dammit!" she breathed, before dashing off.

The layout of the exhibit didn't much help her in the search. The normally brightly lit corridors of the gallery had been replaced by a dimmed installation of soft, suffused lighting that contributed to the ambiance of the theme. Brighter lights were focused only on the portraits themselves, perfectly positioned to highlight the mastery behind the compositions and timing of the snapshots.

The result was that no one within the crowd was immediately recognizable if they didn't stand under the direct glare of that light. Even then, they were only easily distinguishable if they were turned away from the portraits to face the light itself.

Faces swam in and out of her vision, with more than one giving her pause as she mistook them to be either one of the two men who dominated her attention. Five rooms had been dedicated to the display, with four of those surrounding the fifth. The entire gallery had been built to mimic an ancient Roman domus, with the central room acting as an atrium that opened into the four others that surrounded it. The atrium housed the portraits of photographers that had instilled themselves as generous benefactors to the gallery. But the commercialized nature of the privilege went unseen.

A bar had also been set up toward the back, and with that central space leading into the open courtyard beyond, it created the perfect assembly point for speeches and social gatherings. That area, at least, was better lit, but few people were wading through that space; instead, preoccupied with the entries to the exhibit in the other four rooms. Gareth wasn't in any of those, and she hoped by some stroke of luck that his curiosity had found himself in the garden.

It was a beautiful night. The dimmed interior to the gallery contributed to the visibility of the starry sky. To her surprise, a great number of people had made themselves comfortable in the courtyard, mingling with drinks and fine flirtations as new talent made nice with either investors or new clientele.

To her relief, she spotted Gareth standing close to the central fountain. He was looking around, admiring the attention to detail of everything from the trimmed hedges to the garden statues that adorned the walkways. He had the drink he fetched earlier in his hand, and she realized he must have gotten sidetracked. Some part of her found it endearing, but given the circumstances, his proclivity for distraction was proving costly. She couldn't allow her irritation to show, however, or else he would grow suspicious.

"I've been wondering where you wandered off to," she said amicably.

"Huh...oh, geez. Sorry. I've always walked past this gallery, never finding a chance to come and visit. Now I'm kind of wowed by everything. There you go," he handed her the drink.

"It is pretty impressive. Hey…I'm sorry for doing this, but we have to leave. There's an old colleague of mine that I would like to avoid."

He looked over at her, frowning in confusion. "O—kay. Isn't it a bit weird to skip out on an entire evening celebrating some of your work just because there's someone you don't like to see?"

"We have a complicated…business history. I'm afraid they're going to make some trouble tonight."

"So, why not handle it when it happens. I've seen some of your work. You're fucking amazing. Is it fair to yourself to allow someone else to undercut your success like that?"

Fuck, he's beginning to make this too complicated. "Listen, I appreciate that you care enough about my stuff to defend the way you are, but I am just dealing with this the way I see best. There's more to this that you don't know. I'll tell you on the way out of here."

From the look on his face, she could tell he wasn't buying it. She wouldn't either. "So tell me right now," he demanded.

"Gareth. Not now. In the car," she said with more seriousness.

"No. I don't think so. You're not the type to be thrown off by just one person. There's something you're not telling me." He was skeptical and immovable. She realized it was going to be impossible to stir him unless he found good enough reason to. At that moment, his eyes rose from her to look at her back. Her heart nearly sank. They had been running out of time debating to leave. All the while, her back felt exposed everywhere she turned, and she was already starting to get restless of who might surprise her from the blindside.

"Sam! Thank God. I couldn't find him. I— Oh...hey! Ahem. You must be Gareth. My name is Blanche." Sam's friend was visibly nervous. It was clear to anyone that something was up. Even her own palms were starting to feel hot.

"Pleased to meet you." Gareth smiled, doing a far better job at visibly diffusing his suspicion. His demeanor had changed though, and Sam could see how his grip on his glass had almost become white-knuckled.

Blanche did not know what to do with herself. She looked anxiously at Sam for some direction. Suddenly, her eyes widened with a look of abject terror. She didn't need to ask to have her worst fear confirmed.

"Samantha?" the deep sonorous voice came to her from behind.

He walked toward them, illuminated from beneath only by the walkway lights. His imposing figure cast an ominous shadow against the surrounding shrubbery, and his face was all but concealed until he stood right among them. She saw right through his feigned surprise and caught the familiar play of predatory features behind the facade.

"Emilio," her acknowledgment of him was icy, and Gareth didn't miss the forced detachment she displayed.

"God, I haven't seen you in years." He moved in, pulling her forcibly into an embrace. Every cell in her body protested, but yet, she didn't find herself resisting. Pressed against him as she was, the woody scent of his cologne drifted up to meet her. Part of her melted in that embrace then, while another part urged her to push away. The hug, which lasted a small eternity, finally ended. Their eyes lingered on that of the other before his eyes shifted side to side to regard her companions.

"When I saw your name mentioned in this year's emerging artist's line-up, I had to come and see for myself. I was in the city, and a business partner of mine mentioned his involvement in the event. Curiosity got the better of me."

Of course. Resisting the urge to stir trouble usually got the better of you. "I'm flattered," she responded, sounding even more disingenuous than she intended.

"You should be. Your work is brilliant." Gareth's comment felt like a rock shattering glass. The sound immediately shifted the attention, and all eyes were on him as he walked forward with a stalwart and confident grace.

Emilio was the first to speak, his charm slightly affected as he started to take Gareth into consideration.

"I've been telling her that for years. I used to keep the most striking portrait of one of her earlier collections in the home me and Sam shared. One year into our relationship, she really set the standard for birthday gifts."

Samantha remembered that portrait. She also knew why he liked it. The photograph in question had been a nude portrait of Emilio. The play of draping and shadow and highlights had done much to accentuate his physique. The lighting she had chosen that day had bathed him in an amber glow that made him appear almost divine and celestial. It had captured someone of immense beauty but failed to highlight the narcissism that lay skin-deep just beneath the surface. Samantha was repulsed by the work years after.

The tension that had settled in their company could be cut with a knife at that point. Samantha couldn't help but notice as the color drained from Blanche's face. She, like Sam herself, knew that Emilio's recollection had basically surmised their entire history. She looked to Gareth then and saw him keeping his composure in light of the new knowledge. He was new to her, alien in so many ways. Still, she recognized the tension that set in his demeanor as if she had known what it meant for years.

"Well, then. I'd love to see what the future holds. I'm sure some of your best work is still to come," Gareth spared a glance for her momentarily and then turned back to face Emilio.

"My apologies," Emilio started, seething beneath the surface. "I didn't introduce myself. Emilio Bianchi." He held his hand out in greeting.

Things seemed to move in slow motion then. Gareth's drink shifted hands, and Samantha half expected him to offer an introduction in return. Instead, his free hand moved to rest on her lower back. She found herself leaning into that gesture, for both comfort and reassurance. With that single motion, he had made his position in relation to her clear. Emilio noticed, and the effect was immediate.

"Pleased to meet you, Emilio," he answered.

He never offered his name in return. It was the ultimate offense.

The only pleasure that Gareth received in that meeting was taking note of his opposition. Everything else had become a challenge.

In a matter of minutes, Samantha Claremont unwittingly found herself at the cusp of an ancient rivalry. She was the object of interest between two men who vied for her attention. In some self-indulgent way, she was living out some fantasy she once entertained. Was this not what every girl dreamed of? But at the moment, with the pulsating moments of silence marking the manner in which two men took measure of one another, she was struggling to bring herself to feel thrilled in any way.

Blanche looked about ready to die. At first, Samantha didn't notice that she even had a drink in her hand. Neither did she notice how quickly it had been emptied. The nerves were clearly getting the better of some of them.

Emilio and Gareth continued their silent tug-of-war. One of them had her heart once. The other was starting to win it over. She realized then, how little credit she had given Gareth for his ability to project his dominance. For years, Emilio had been the epitome of masculine prowess in her experience. No one could stand against him in her mind. But under the fiery gaze of her ex, Gareth was proving himself to be an immovable object.

"Sam. I think it's time we left," he said, moving his hand around her waist as a silent gesture to walk away.

"You've hardly finished your drink," Emilio commented, the amusement in his voice cracking in the onslaught of his jealousy.

"The company doesn't do it justice, I'm afraid," Gareth made a motion to leave, nudging Sam gently to walk ahead. She didn't retaliate.

They were a few paces away when his voice followed them. "I hope to see you again, Sam. I'll be around for some time."

She cringed inward at the final comment, and against her better judgment, she turned around. The look in his eye confirmed to her that his comment was more than it appeared to be on the surface. As she faced forward again, she couldn't shake the feeling that this was far from over.

***

The silence in the car ride home was deafening. Sam looked over at Gareth a couple of times, hoping to at least start a conversation. By some cruel trick, his glasses kept obscuring his eyes, reflecting only the passing lights of the city. He never looked more unapproachable then. His mouth was set in a tight line. His jaw was tense. He was brooding and volatile and it made her unnerved as to what to do. It was obvious that he was processing the run-in they had at the gallery.

After a good number of minutes, Samantha couldn't take it anymore.

"Ok, look. Things are tense. I get it. But you can't give me the silent treatment."

"We did talk," he started, nearly making her heart stop with the immediacy by which he offered an answer. "And then the circumstances became self-evident." It was as though he had gone through the conversation in his mind and knew exactly what he wanted to say.

"I'm sorry," was all she got out. "That must have been uncomfortable for you."

"The only thing that made me uncomfortable was your dishonesty about your relationship. A colleague? C'mon Sam. That was a bad lie. It grossly underestimated the gravity of the situation."

"It was the only thing I could think of that would make you leave with me."

"Why would we have left? I said so once, I'll say it again. You're supposed to be there."

"You saw how intense that was. If I didn't know any better, I would have sworn the two of you would have a go at each other."

"You've got to give me more credit than that. I don't pick fights with the self-absorbed alpha types unless I need to."

"He *is* the alpha type Gareth. He makes sport out of taunting other men just to prove it."

"To what end? Why does he need to prove it that much? If you ask me, there is a deeply hidden insecurity that must be playing out to make him act that way. He isn't worth my time." He was strangely serene as he acknowledged the fact. It confused her because it failed to match his stoic and moody demeanor that she had been struggling to place.

"I don't understand. In saying that, you don't seem entirely upset. And a moment ago, you seemed almost detached when I thought you were angry with me. Yet, something is off. I just can't figure out what. It's clearly not what I thought it was."

"I'm not mad at you Samantha. You left me a bit unprepared, but it wasn't as grueling in the end. And as I said: he may be formidable as far as men go, but he's not infallible. I don't feel intimidated." She believed him. Every word he said was truthful. But there was definitely more to it.

"Then what is it?"

"He's still a threat."

"You just said he didn't scare you off."

"He doesn't. But you saw the way he looked at you. No one said it out loud, but I know he's your ex. You may have moved on, but he doesn't look like a man that has made peace with his past. He wants you back—badly. I don't think you comprehend exactly how serious he is. You didn't see—maybe you couldn't—but from the very moment I made it clear that I wasn't going anywhere, the chinks in his armor were revealed."

"Emilio is...persistent. That I'll give you. But I'd doubt he'd do anything crazy while here."

He was quiet for a moment and didn't answer immediately.

"I'm not entirely convinced. There's something you need to know about men like him, something that I don't think you would have noticed in your relationship. Men like that wear masks all the time. You may have seen one of them in all the time you've spent together, but you never saw which one he donned when you walked out of this relationship—which I assume you did."

"Yeah. I walked away from all of it."

"Well, I saw another side of it tonight. You may have gotten a glimpse of it as well. He had the look of a man who has committed himself to a sole purpose: getting you back."

"There's little he can do that will win me back over."

"He's not going to *win* you back. Sam, he intends to *take* you. The outcome is already clear in his mind. He doesn't care how he accomplishes that, or what the consequences will be for what he's willing to do. There is only one way he walks away from this, and that is with you by his side. Once he saw me as an obstacle in that objective, it was the unspoken truth that he made clear when I looked him in the eye."

His words fell on her ears like an ominous portent. Somehow, it became evident that she had underestimated the situation. She had put much of the past behind her, intent on burying the chaotic years spent in finding herself in a relationship that never truly served her. At most, she wanted to avoid the run-in with her ex, seeing it as nothing more than an uncomfortable drawback. Now, she wondered whether they were facing a bigger complication.

"You're being very quiet."

"I'm thinking…"

"About?"

"Well dammit, Gareth. Isn't it obvious? A few nights ago I answered to no one but myself. Now I'm in between a rock and a hard place."

"You're…conflicted?"

"Yes."

He went silent again, and clearly, her words had landed differently than she intended.

"Sam, if you're conflicted, then that must mean he still gets a reaction from you. Do you still have feelings for him?"

Her impulse was to say no, but that wasn't her immediate reaction. She hesitated, and it was enough of an answer. Gareth pursed his lips in reaction. He wasn't an idiot. If anything, he was as capable as she was in reading people's true emotions behind the words they chose to use. But did she really have unresolved feelings? Were some of them so subliminal that it had taken her a clash of wills to see it for what it was? It must be. It was all there, in the seconds that ticked by where she didn't have an answer for him.

Gareth was diplomatic and instead chose to change the subject.

"Tell me about him. About the relationship you had."

"Right now?"

"It's as good a time as any. There were too many moments of uncertainty back there, and too much in between to instigate it. All of it remained unspoken. So I figured something big must have happened. Taking that it made me feel protective, even defensive, tells me that I've come to care about you enough to have to start considering what might be standing in my way."

She had to smile, not because what he said was in any way funny, but simply because it set butterflies loose in her stomach.

"If I didn't know any better, I'd say that sounded like you wanted to put up a fight for me?"

His answer was definitive.

"Hell yes!"

Chapter 7:
Warning Labels

Emilio Bianchi.

Long ago, the name was like a rapture on the tongue. Sam would never forget how people dropped his name in near orgasmic pleasure. Women found him irresistible, while men wrestled with a mixture of idolization and envy. Her grandmother had once said that young marriages ended spontaneously whenever a Bianchi man was in town. Some never made it to the wedding.

The Bianchis were a notoriously powerful Italian family who had settled in the Hamptons. It wasn't long before they ingratiated themselves among the rich families of the community. Suave and courteous, the sons of every generation seemed blessed with an unfathomable beauty that made each one of them objects of great desire. Every godly trope that had attached itself to the Bianchi name was not ill-begotten. In time, as they married among the elite single women of the various families, money inevitably became another symbol that was tied to them. Millionaire playboys became but one of the many labels that were thrown around.

Growing up in the nestled comfort of affluence, any daughter from the east side of Manhattan envied a little taste of danger when it came their way. Years later, Sam found it strange that the mothers would never warn their children of the heartache that inevitably followed an involvement with a Bianchi bad boy. The sins of old were repeated again and again, and many found themselves later in marriages that only ever scratched the surface of that same excitement.

Samantha didn't open herself to such disillusion. Even at 20, she was not a plucky girl that could be strung along by fanciful ideals.

Every family inevitably belonged to a number of exclusive clubs, each of which regularly organized social gatherings between the affiliated families. She was forced to attend many of them, in the hopes that the networking involved would ultimately yield attractive opportunities—for both her career and potential matchmaking.

She attended, feeling starry-eyed by such agenda-driven events as a teen, and bored thereof as she stepped from adolescence into adulthood. Becoming a tycoon, or marrying one, never appealed to her. She was a rebel, driven by the lust for creative and leftist pursuits instead of influence.

Nevertheless, she attended dutifully as a Claremont, bent on carving out her own future. She feigned friendliness among shallow company and surprisingly did find meaningful connections for opportunities in the future. But she wanted the grittier life that existed outside of the stagnant ideals of the rich.

That is when Emilio crossed her path.

The youngest of his family, he was a son of the bloodline that both fit every stereotype and then crushed it as he saw fit. He was a rebel with a cause, cut from a different cloth. He inherited his family's insatiable appetite for power but decided on his own course of action to obtain it.

They were two children, of two distinctive families, breaking the mold of tradition secretly. They saw eye to eye immediately.

Things fell into place instantaneously, against the better judgments of their respective families. Emilio was born into enough money to start his own business at a young age, founding multiple entrepreneurial ventures that yielded great success, while amazingly keeping the details thereof concealed from his father. Sam had secreted away a scholarship for studies abroad, relinquishing her inheritance to pursue her passion. In an instant, they had cut themselves loose from family dependence and struck out into the world. They left behind familial expectations, old social circles, and the gated lifestyle of people who were nothing more than systemic aristocrats. To all else, they appeared to have eloped. In truth, they were nothing more than young people trying to make their own way.

Their escapades took them to Paris, where she attended l'École Nationale Supérieure des Beaux-Arts, an astute art school. Emilio found his way in e-commerce, a side-hustle that exploded when he redirected his time and energy to fully commit himself to the venture.

For a time, everything was idyllic. They were in one of the most beautiful cities in the world. Their careers were growing, both of them becoming entrenched in separate crafts. The once-proud legacies of their family names became inconsequential, no longer seeming to cast a looming shadow on their individual paths.

Looking back, Samantha could never deny that they were madly in love. Emilio was Sam's first challenge, whilst she was the only one he ever faced. Young, free, and talented...the world was at their feet. And sometimes, especially in those first years of their relationship, Emilio seemed to be at hers. His adoration was evident in every gesture, every touch, and every lingering look.

And the sex was great.

She remembered the first time he had taken her, the night after they had met. He had kissed her breathlessly all the way into one of the many guest rooms of his family estate. In that labyrinth of a house, he assured her of their privacy as they gave in to their cravings. He slipped her out of her dress as if he had done so a million times. He found every sweet spot effortlessly, taking her into the tender wilderness of toe-curling pleasure as he proved his expertise in driving a woman wild.

They fell in an intertwined heap on the bed. Her fingers dug furrows into his strong back as his hot breath pulsed down her neck. Moans turned into silent gestures of wide-mouthed ecstasy as she writhed under his touch. Just as she thought he had exhausted his efforts on nearly every part of her anatomy, he hovered over her.

His skin glistened in the pale light that shone through the window, taut over the hard muscle that coiled around every part of his perfect figure. She was ensconced in his strong embrace, desperate to feel him inside of her. He must have seen it then, her want for him. It was a defining moment, Samantha had told herself.

In his mind, Emilio had seen more in the lustful look she gave him that night; more so than she had warranted. Her attraction was undeniable, that much was true. She was fully mindful, wanting it more even as she was living right through it. But men see things differently...even the masterpiece that was Emilio. He took that longing stare as a conviction of her affection, an unbreakable tie that soul bonded them forever. In his mind,

Emilio had convinced himself that she was his; that she *always* would be. And with that fantasy entrenching itself in his mind, he made love to her.

It lasted hours. It always did. In his wild passion alone, he had become somewhat of a muse for her art. They could never extinguish their burning desire, and every time their bodies met, it carried something of a residual glimmer of that first time. They wanted more. They always wanted more. There was something celestial about the subject of your first infatuation. Every physical collision of hormonally-charged molecules felt like an otherworldly experience.

Given, their spurts with marijuana opened their minds to heightened encounters.

But even great lovemaking alone couldn't save what their relationship would become. He was still a Bianchi, and soon the family legacy inevitably reared its ugly head.

Clandestine business meetings soon provoked her suspicion, and an entire backlog of black-market dealings revealed themselves to her through a history of encrypted and hidden messages she stumbled upon while scrolling through one of his devices. He didn't react well to her discovery and assumed even more hidden agendas and skulking behavior in an effort to evade her attention.

His narrative of success had bred a sense of entitlement to the type of luxuries life afforded them. Ironically, it restricted their freedoms once again, making them move among similar types of people they had escaped back home.

Everything that followed seemed to her nearly as anxiety-provoking. She couldn't remember what came next. Months followed in a blur of illicit deals, lies, and even drugs. Perhaps she could have survived it, endured it even in the hopes that somehow he could be fixed. But then the emotional abuse began.

He never demeaned or insulted her. He wasn't the type. He was crazy for her after all, and beyond that, her self-esteem had developed well beyond the constant validation needed from others. Instead, he hid his wrongdoing by manipulating the truth. He did it to such an extent, that she began to question her own reality.

The gaslighting continued for as long as she carried suspicion of all his crimes. He chipped away at her sanity, piece by piece, to thicken the smokescreens he threw up in an attempt to conceal his dealings. His fervent and flagrant denials of the truth made her stop every time she was convinced that she was getting closer to the truth.

It carried on for five years, the damage of which remained unseen as they ventured more and more into the glitzy lives of celebrities and the oligarchy. Sometimes, it seemed to her as though they kept up the appearance of a glamorous young couple set to impress the social circles they moved in. But on the inside, Samantha, at least, felt like a shadow of the person she had once been or even hoped to become.

She was convinced it would end there. Emilio had carved enough notches in the wall of his achievements. He became a force to be reckoned with, and she could not fathom a man craving more power than he already had.

His neuroticism proved her wrong. It began with a passing glance from a bachelor, one of many they came across in the parties they hosted or attended. Jealousy clawed like a maddened beast at his mind, and every man became a threat.

He started looking for the nonverbal cues to fuel his suspicion. Every time another man looked, talked, or touched her, it became the topic of another confrontation, and later on a vicious argument.

In a way, it had been one of those horrible blessings in disguise. His delusions started convincing her that she may have never been the crazy one. Steadily, she climbed out of the slump of the reality that had been warped for her and saw past the blinders of her devotion to him.

One night, the breaking point came, and his jealousy uncaged a wild animal. He came home with another one of his accusations. Drunk and delusional, he started throwing things around. Her love for him had steadily withered for months. At that moment, it shattered to the melody of breaking glass, and tumbling furniture, and finally died when she looked into his eye.

He never lifted a hand against her. But right then, she almost expected him too.

The choices before her seemed simple, so she took the one he least expected.

She left.

She never stayed long enough to find out what part had been most surprising to him: the fact that their 'forever after' had ended, or the fact that she was capable of slipping away as easily as she did. Perhaps his love for her had blinded him. He underestimated her capabilities, believing he had her trapped in the gridlock of his deceit, financial control, and appeal.

But she paid attention. She had full knowledge of their shared assets and any other finances that tied them together. With the many covert dealings he had done, she could walk away with all their capital that was considered legal. And...they were never married.

But she only took only what she needed, silently sneaking away through her own connections and the quick wit that was a staple of the Claremont name. But once she got out, she decided to run. Her mind had played through a million scenarios of what that last night could become, and she was not about to let victimhood number as one of the possibilities. She knew Emilio in and out and had managed to see through him, but she couldn't be sure of what he'd do next.

He was dashing, rich, powerful, unstable, and unpredictable.

She was clever.

She found her way back to New York then, relieved to be back in a space that was familiar, but one she would certainly experience differently after being away for years. She reconnected, rebuilt, and realigned her purposes, and steadily found herself on track again.

Her family absorbed her almost immediately. To some extent, she believed it to be tactical. In that first year back, a slight paranoia tugged at her mind concerning her safety. Emilio's underground deals had inevitably made him befriend a number of unsavory characters. She never knew when one of them might make an uncanny appearance at his behest. Her father, peaceful and beneficent as he was, could be equally ruthless. Her mother proved just as formidable. Samantha always thought Daphne Claremont would be able to fulfill her role as mob wife with fierce dedication. In the end, reestablishing the ties with her family offered her protection. The fact that they found her first as she re-entered the Manhattan spheres proved a saving grace to counter many sleepless nights.

Samantha never clung to the past for too long, and soon any notion of fear or regret evaporated in the onslaught of her success. She was a thriving bachelorette that didn't need to answer to anyone—at least in non-traditional senses. She established endearing friendships, a dynamic career, and a notable reputation that opened up many doors.

She was the first Claremont that had reinvented the wheel, and her family assimilated her success without question. Though they'd never admit it, Samantha had no doubt that her parents were overjoyed to see the return of the prodigal daughter. Her mother had gained a mature companion, and her father had regained a legacy.

All areas of her life were gravitating toward some version of the happiness she had envisioned for herself, more than half a decade ago. But her notions of romance still seemed tainted.

She never stepped into a serious relationship again. Nor, when she reflected on it, did she ever truly date. She was not closed off to the flirtations and advances of other men, and her bed had seen more than one stranger for single overnight delights. But none of those harked back to the thrill and excitement she had with Emilio.

Most times, their personalities were one-dimensional. There was nothing beyond the chiseled physiques or the charming social playbooks that some had to offer. The sex was mediocre, lacking in that eye-rolling pleasure that defined those long nights spent in a lover's arms.

She enjoyed being single again. The freedoms that it permitted her were underrated. Without the expectations of mutual choices holding her back, she was capable of pursuing life by the beat of her own drum.

Yet, Samantha found herself longing for companionship. Shallow admiration, one-night-stands, and men falling short of expectations simply weren't adding value to her life. She didn't need validation, neither was she addicted to it. There was simply something immensely satisfying in the way a man looked at you as if you were the only woman that existed in the world.

She yearned for Emilio then, in those long and sleepless nights that found her tossing and turning with reminiscence. She groped between empty sheets, searching for the hard contours of a body that was carved by a Renaissance master. She missed the splash of his dark hair over the pillows, the five-o-clock shadow that sculpted his face, and the way his sleeping complexion softened features always carved in hard determination. She thought back on the thousand philosophical ramblings that used to fill those restless hours when neither of them could find peace in the night. And then, perhaps most of all, she missed the raw and unapologetic masculine energy that surrounded him.

Her reflections stopped in those moments. Without realizing it then, in those first years of recovery after stepping out of that life, Emilio had become the archetype in her mind for the perfect man. Flawed as he was, the complex nexus of his character had no comparison. Every other man would always fall short of his prowess and intensity.

So she went out, looking to find herself. She found herself with men who kept on reminding her of what she was lacking. Her mother had warned her then, of the inappropriateness of her behavior. Her exploits on the playing field of the eligibles ran the risk of attracting the wrong kind of attention. Not to mention, that every man leaving her apartment was another segment of salacious stories that could be told of the Claremont progeny.

But Samantha kept on toying with fate, telling her mother that she was not bound to the faded glory of the rich. She kept on casting her line, seeing what fish in the sea were brave enough to take a bite. In truth, she acknowledged that a part of her wanted to relive the high she got from her previous relationship. She had turned herself into a serial hookup, desperately trying to get a stronger and stronger fix that could satiate her desires.

A woman realizes then the types of scars a man is capable of leaving, even years after their absence. A woman realizes what scars she self-inflicts as well.

Samantha had been the one to walk away and she had to bear the weight of her decision. More days than not, she would consider the wisdom of that choice, reprimanding herself for it afterward. If anything, she prided herself in owning up to her actions. The reasons for her exit were substantial, and she could only imagine the consequences of staying in the toxic space their relationship had become.

Still, despite that wisdom, the very notion to long for her old life told her that deep down she may have become addicted to a dangerous man.

***

Bit by bit, she mapped out the history with her ex, keeping parts to herself she believed Gareth would prefer not knowing.

He listened to each detail intently, at times squinting as if to withstand the glare of some of her confessions. She cringed inwardly as well, speaking about Emilio with such adulation at times. Nevertheless, he persisted, managing to sit through the long drawl of not only the facts but her feelings about them as well.

They had returned to his place, sitting amid the soft glow of dimmed lamps in his studio apartment. Outside, the city lights created their own galaxy, and it lent something almost mysterious and compelling to her retelling of the past.

In the moment of silence that followed, she wondered how Gareth was taking it all. Some part of him looked hungry for the details. In between her recounting, he had stopped to prod for more. He was constructing a schema of Emilio, assimilating the disparate parts of her memory and his own meeting with her ex. A competitive fire burned in the depths of his eyes and she knew that his desire for knowledge was strategic.

But some, if not most of it, could not have been easy to hear. She had shown her vulnerability to him in the residual feelings that still tied themselves to Emilio. Though Gareth was still new to her, he was fast establishing himself as a fixture in her life. In so many ways, he was not at all the man she had been looking for. In so many others, he was proving to be the man that she didn't know she needed.

He was gentle, calm, and balanced, and within that balance resided another lethality that came from something very unexpected: self-control. He knew himself, all too well, and premeditated the fights where his strengths could come in handy, or his weaknesses stand in his way. Those same equations were operating in his mind right now, as he measured himself against another man.

"Say something," she coaxed, desperate to know his thoughts.

"Not yet," he answered.

"You've been staring at the carpet forever. It's driving me nuts."

"It's just new to you," he said, giving her a knowing look over the rims of his glasses. "I think that you're not used to relinquishing control," he added, just slightly amused.

"*I* told you that. Pfft. Some nerve you have using my self-insights against me," she said, in an effort to break the tension.

"It's those self-insights that's the hardest to retaliate against," he challenged.

"Drop it, Wakeford. You already have the upper hand in this situation. I basically bore my heart on my sleeve for you just then."

"I know," he said more demurely. "I'm just teasing you." He stood up and walked to stand over by the large window overlooking the city.

"I know—it's difficult to hear. Frankly, I was beginning to distance myself from old feelings. It was just a slow process. I don't think five years disappear as easily in three. At best, it's all a weaning process."

"He's a magnetic man, and you've been struggling for some time to shift polarity. I get it."

"Wow. I wish I had that line when I went to see the therapist."

He swung around, looking surprised, "*You* went for relationship advice?"

"Hmph. I saw many. You might even say I went therapist shopping at one point. None of them lasted past the first session. I guess I never needed advice. I just needed someone to listen. I think I wanted to hear myself telling the story. Every time I told it, I learned something new."

"Well then, here's a question for you. What is it you want?"

Jesus, that's a tough question, she thought. "Most people spend their whole lives figuring that out you know."

"Well, yeah. You're not wrong. It's because our wants go through stages. But you only go through those stages when you reach them. So I'm talking about what you want right now." His tone was becoming progressively serious, and she couldn't help but feel unsettled as to where this conversation would lead.

"You're wondering...where *you* fit in."

"Is that an unfair question?"

"No. It's not." She just didn't know what more to tell him.

"Now you're the one being quiet," he prodded.

"Look, Gareth, you're smart. Trying to fool you about how past feelings are affecting me is a waste of time. What you need to know, is that any feelings I have left are fading. After all that I've been through, I can't go back. There's no reason for that. Right now, *this* is reality. How we choose to react to it is entirely our prerogative."

The city lights illuminated one side of his face in his steady contemplation.

"Emilio isn't going away soon you know. I don't think it will be as easy to brush him aside. We're still going to see a lot of him." His words were a reminder, even a warning.

"All the more reason you need to help me to keep perspective," she said softly. There was something seductive to the way she said it. It was a subconscious slip that perhaps communicated a deeper need given their present situation.

He must have noticed, for he walked over then, and kissed her fervently. Then another night was spent in bodily surrender.

Chapter 8:
Putting Playthings Away

The call rattled her awake.

Samantha nearly rolled off the couch. The book she'd been reading fell to the floor and she reached for the phone while fighting through the drowsiness. It took her a second or two to register the name on the display, before feeling disgruntled as she answered.

"Hi, Mom."

"Sam, darling, I've been trying to get a hold of you the entire day. Are you still awake?"

"I am now," she sighed. *The entire day, she says.* Sam did notice a single missed call after work, but she had decided to deal with her mother in the morning. It was clear her evasive tactic hadn't worked. "What's up?"

"Father and I want to discuss something with you. Explaining it now will be a bit of a hassle, but I was thinking you could come around for dinner tomorrow night."

"It's in the middle of the week, though. I appreciate the invitation, but could we maybe rather schedule it for the weekend?" Samantha definitely wasn't feeling up to sitting through a Claremont dinner while she was trying to get through the mid-week slump. Work had been hectic, and after being surrounded by people the entire day, she wanted nothing more than to be alone. Besides that, Gareth was coming over.

Though she refrained from mentioning that on the call.

"I'm afraid it's rather an urgent conversation, dear. It really cannot wait. Come around at 7:30." Daphne Claremont simply hung up after that, probably content that she would inevitably have her way.

***

The next morning, Samantha woke up with a strange sense of foreboding. To shake it off, she went for a jog in the hopes that it would clear her head. It was a beautiful sunny day, but it didn't do much to uplift her spirits. She just couldn't shake the suspicion that her evening was about to send her life into some upheaval.

She'd been too disgruntled the previous night by her mother's call to actually process the faint apprehension. Suddenly, it was gnawing at her mind. So she gave up the jog altogether, deciding that she'd sprint back and start her day. Perhaps work could get her mind off things.

And for a time, it really did. The work with *Fashion Digest* was constant and all-consuming, taking up most of her time and energy. She found herself fully immersed in the role of creative director to the layout of the fall shoot, even though she wasn't the one paid to do so. The contract with Fae Mayweather had, however, promised some handsome stipends for her additional involvement, and she was more than willing to comply to see her vision executed from the shoot, right down to the printed page.

After the day, she stumbled into her home. She was exhausted but had worked much of the anxiety out of her system. Whatever the sudden urgency was by which her parents were driven to see her would inevitably come to pass. It wasn't something she could control. She just couldn't imagine what it could possibly be.

An evening at the Claremont estate had the naturally built-in expectation that all in attendance were to dress their best. It was as though they were the modern equivalent to an aristocracy, with a set of day and evening wear ready for whatever the occasion called for. So after a shower and a stress-provoking pensive moment in front of her wardrobe, she finally left the house in a simple red number and heels in hand, with the tip of a cardigan clenched between her teeth as she tried to gather herself between keys. Clothing and accessories. *If mom were to see me now,* she thought.

Rushed as she sometimes was, she had long since mastered the art of applying make-up on the drive. Blush, lipstick, and mascara flitted between her hand and the glove compartment, right up till the moment of her last application in front of her family home. That was when she noticed another car. It was a black Bentley, definitely not one belonging to either of her parents. *Was there someone else attending dinner then?* She didn't know anyone in her family's social network well enough to know what they drove, but it immediately told her that the dynamic of the evening would not at all correlate to her expectation.

Nevertheless, she shrugged it off and walked up to the front door. Her mother answered almost immediately, as per usual. Daphne always sported an immaculate pompadour in the 1940s fashion. Her face was cast in that most stern of expressions, determined and unreadable, and dusted off with the finest cosmetics. With a pressed dress and the attitude to wear it, she gave her daughter an almost mechanical acknowledgment as she welcomed her inside. Samantha could only venture to guess what her mother may have thought of her own look. She wasn't nearly as polished and refined.

"Glad you made it, dear."

"Well, you know, I was *summoned*," Samantha replied snidely. She didn't look at her mother's expression, instead, looking down the hallway to where her father peeked around the corner. Tom Claremont was much less frigid than his wife, and whereas she could keep her emotions from playing on her features, Tom had no such talent.

"Hey, dad." Samantha knew something was off immediately. He tried to force a smile, but he looked pained and even distressed. It immediately raised red flags.

"Hello, Samantha," he said, his voice cracking slightly at the end.

She felt her mother's hand come to rest on her shoulder. "Let's move to the living area. Dinner should be ready in another 20 minutes. We can chat till then."

Samantha's legs moved on their own accord, even though she resisted taking a step further. She began to feel unsettled again, and her stomach turned at the thought of what awaited her in the other room.

"So, apparently the two of you have something urgent to discuss?"

Neither of them answered as they walked into the dining hall, which flanked the living space just beyond. The silence was provocative of some hidden agenda and she wondered when her parents had become such masters of suspense.

As a lone figure stood at the mantelpiece of their unlit fireplace, she also wondered when they had become such curators of horror.

Hearing footsteps behind him, Emilio Bianchi turned and flashed the dazzling smile that disarmed with malevolent intent. He looked every bit like the younger version of his father then, dressed in a bespoke suit that seemed like he was about to swindle you out of your last shred of dignity. His swept-back, shoulder-length hair made the unyielding look in his eyes all the more threatening. But her parents would never see that part. No. He hid that under a thousand layers of charm and deceit that made his handsome face as compelling as the words he used to have his way.

"Evening, Samantha. You look ravishing as ever."

Of course, I do. I would look exquisite in a trash bag if you knew you had the upper hand.

"Emilio. I didn't expect to see you here."

"Emilio's been back in the city for quite some time, honey," her mother remarked.

Honey. Would you just listen to that? The term of endearment was new for her mother, whose form of address to you was always so rife with formality that you were left wondering if there was anything that could thaw that glacial personality. This newfound affection was all a front. She wasn't buying it. It didn't hide the deceit that was evident this night.

"You don't say?" she faked.

"He said he bumped into you the other when you were among colleagues of yours. You never got around to talking."

Colleagues, huh? Interesting word choice, considering he knew exactly what the relational dynamic was. Come now, Emilio. You can surely think of better ways to cope with your jealousy.

"That's why your mother was so kind as to invite me to dinner," Emilio said, plastering the charm all over his smug face.

"You don't say?" Samantha feigned interest. "Where did you come across each other then?"

"Oh well, your father and Stefano had a business meeting the other day. Emilio happened to tag along."

Stefano Bianchi. It was Emilio's older brother. It was no coincidence that he stepped in on the scene. Emilio and Stefano were nearly inseparable. He wouldn't hesitate to zealously stand in defense of his younger sibling. If he was involved, then this business meeting was a smokescreen to a much larger ploy. She didn't know how much the brothers were aligned in their purposes, but she could almost certainly venture a guess as to what Emilio aimed to get out of it.

"Wine, dear? I got your favorite," her mother almost crooned.

"Hmm. Oh yes. Thank you." She was being distracted by her internal dialogue, but she saw no other way to get through their situation. She was surprised when her mother pulled forth a *Groot Constantia* Sauvignon Blanc from the ice bucket. She didn't know how she acquired it or where she even kept it all that time, but in cracking open a South African label on a night such as this, Sam could only imagine what was in store for her.

"Well now," her mother started as she handed Samantha her glass. "Why don't we all make our way to the table. "Emilio...Sam, you sit on the opposite sides there. Your father and I will sit at the table's ends."

Thank God, Sam thought. The idea of sitting right next to him had appalled her. She even suspected such a duplicitous gesture from her mother. But across from him, she could do better to manage the situation. She may have been grossly unprepared at their previous encounter, distracted by the others. But here, the battlefield was equalized. True, that they were at her mother's dinner table. Under her roof, manners trumped all personal squabbles and trifles. It did mean that she needed to watch herself. But if Emilio thought he had the upper hand, he made a serious miscalculation. He would have to walk the line of polite formality, and she was willing to place bets on how long she thought he'd be able to endure it.

"Emilio," her father started, turning to him as they all took their seats, "we never did manage to talk about what brings you back to America."

Samantha noticed her mother flinch ever so slightly, composing herself right before her eyes threw daggers at her husband. *Odd,* Sam thought, *that dad would ask that question. It's almost like he didn't even know about this dinner.* The realization struck her with a force. The question then was a challenge. A subtle one, but nonetheless enough to allow his daughter some ammunition.

To say that Sam was disappointed that her father allowed this evening to even happen would have been an understatement. From her mother, she would expect it, but she and her father had spent many nights talking of the past, finding that she had confided in him more than she ever dreamed possible. Even though he dissociated from most of the drama in his life, Sam did feel that her father cared deeply about her. He just had an odd way of showing it, much like tonight. He redeemed himself then by proving that he didn't know. Otherwise, he would've never posed the question.

The food arrived, carried in by the staff. She regretted the timing, purely because it bought Emilio some time. Before that moment, he had floundered momentarily, but only long enough for her to see that he wasn't in full command of his emotions.

"Since launching my platform for e-commerce, I've not only attracted clients, but also people who were keen to learn the trade. About two years ago I launched a mentorship program to train students in the ins-and-outs of everything related to the business model. A lot of them are in America, coincidentally. Many of them have given life to start-ups with great potential that I'd like to further invest in, but I needed to be here for some of the process. I'd thought to see the family while I was here as well. It's been many years." His answer was smooth, calculated, and valid. Enough to douse the fires of any suspicion.

"I'm sure it has. You've never seen any of them since?" *Classic Daphne Claremont.* Ever the diplomat. She knew the history well. Samantha didn't understand her motives. *What game is she playing?*

"No. I'm afraid I haven't. But, they've been well. Papa was especially thrilled to welcome me back. He—"

"How long will you be staying?" Samantha interjected, trying to keep her tone neutral. Still, even she couldn't deny the tinge of coldness that inevitably crept through.

He must have noticed.

"The choice is mine, actually. I have partners that run the business in my stead while I'm away. With all of it online, I can check in when needed, of course. So you might say, I'm staying indefinitely for the time being."

Well, that's just great. She simply nodded, offering a smile so laced with insincerity that she had to concentrate hard enough to just form it.

"Have the two of you kept in contact after all these years?" her father asked as he looked at the two of them from beneath hooded brows. He was tentative and unsure. Samantha could empathize. What did a man say at a table with his daughter and the ex-boyfriend that his wife had invited?

"No," Sam answered. "You could say the fault is mine. Seeing Emilio at the gallery the other night was quite a surprise." Her words were seething as left her mouth, and she could almost taste the bitterness of them as their intent lay on her tongue.

"I wouldn't be too hard on myself if I was you, Sam," Emilio responded while cutting into his steak. "We got distracted by many things as our lives complicated themselves." He looked at her with those last words, taking a bite slowly as he watched the effect they had on her. The comment was general enough to avoid attention, but each word he used was carefully chosen. She knew it was a subtle jab to the choices she had made not only long ago, but recently.

"Fair enough. I happen to like a complicated life, and the distractions I've chosen fall neatly in my preferences." It was a verbal contest, and she was not about to lose to him.

"Sam," her mother interceded, with a tone her daughter knew would shift the balance again. "Emilio made a passive comment the other day that I think could stand as an interesting proposal.

He was talking about your exhibit the other day, and how you could capitalize on your talent by considering an online-consumer base for all your commissions."

"My theory is that an online portfolio could attract a fan base of sorts that could potentially develop into a pool of investors. We can build in a sort of perpetual property rights to your work. That way, you can sell your photographs to them at high profits, while receiving passive income over time as consumers start selling your artwork to the highest bidder. You can make money from the increasing popularity of your name alone."

He probably knew that he was selling himself on a bullshit premise, even though he was wrapping it in grandiose promises.

"Thank you. However, my personal ventures are completely removed from any lucrative means. They are purely artistic."

"Commendable as that is Samantha, Emilio speaks some sense. Emilio's family has an extensive social network to tap into. Maybe they could provide a decent consumer injection to the initiative to increase traffic to the platform. Perhaps it's wise to hear him out on—"

"Thank you, mother," she interrupted. She tried to take the bite out of her tone, but she didn't succeed. "I'm well aware of Emilio's proficiency to build a successful venture. I'm also well aware of his methods." She flashed a look at him as she mentioned the last bit. She cut into her own steak with such ferocity that only the scrape of her utensils against her plate filled the silence that seemed to echo in the room.

They all ate in silence. Samantha found the apathy to the discomfort unbelievable. None of them were fools. Each person at that table knew the gravity that lay between Samantha and her ex, even if to varying degrees. She never remembered having a heart to heart with her mother in all her years since being back. Her father knew and dealt with it in his own way. Sam was well aware of it, feeling the tautness of her anger and apprehension every time a flicker of memory ignited in her mind. As for Emilio…God knew what thoughts he entertained with her sudden, unannounced, and secret departure under the veil of night.

It went on for another five minutes, before Samantha snapped, unable to bear it any more.

"Why did I come tonight? Mother, you mentioned that the matter was urgent."

Her mother stopped chewing, swallowing hard before she set down her utensils, folded her hands in front of her, and assumed the cast of every powerful business woman that was about to enforce their authority.

"I think you know why."

"No, I don't. The reasons completely escaped me while concealed by all the underhanded planning to have my ex sit across from me at the table!" Her voice had nearly raised to a shout, and that uneasy silence had settled once again in its wake. Strangely, Emilio remained silent. It was perhaps the wisest thing he'd done since knowing him. When two Claremont women were at each other's throats, you never intervened.

"I knew you wouldn't come willingly with the knowledge that he'd be here. So some secrets were necessary, yes."

"Daphne, I thought you told Samantha that Emilio would be here. You told me as much when he showed up for dinner," Tom announced.

There it was, Sam thought, *the indisputable proof that mother had been the mastermind behind this fuckery.*

"They need to talk, Tom," Daphne said sternly. "I never knew the reasons behind your separation, or even your return years ago. But I accepted it, believing it was mutual. But, it has come to my attention that you have not been forthcoming with the entire truth."

"What truth do you need, mother?" Samantha managed to get out, her voice pitched as the anger shook her. "It didn't work out. That should be enough."

"You owe him more, Samantha."

"Owe him mo—" she stopped short, directing a fiery glare at Emilio. "What the hell did you tell her?"

"We...spoke openly," he said calmly. "I told her how I felt."

"Ah, yes. Because you were always so forthright about your emotions. Don't be so sanctimonious Bianchi. I think you fabricated a truth that pushed your narrative!"

"Samantha. Calm down! You will compose yourself at my table!"

"*No!* That is quite enough. Listen to me and listen to me well. I don't know what delusion of control you have nurtured over my choices in the years since I've been back, but I will not be talked down to. I deserve more respect than what has been shown to me in your home tonight."

"You've decimated the respect you were owed the minute you brought shame upon us!" her mother bit back.

"*Still?* Are you still so fixated on me being a young woman in love and deciding to break free from this gilded cage to find my own way? It's been eight years, mother. We've all moved on! Please join us in the realm of reality."

"The reality is that you've compromised Bianchis' faith in us! And it is your duty to restore it!" her mother shouted in a shrill voice.

Samantha was stunned and left in a daze. "Wh—what are you talking about? Dad," she said, turning to her father, "what is she talking about?"

"Daphne...?" he implored, as confused as Sam was.

"Tom...we'll leave these two to discuss their matters. I will talk privately with you in your study." She stood up so quickly that the tableware quivered, taking her wine as she stalked off to her father's home office.

"I'm...I'm sorry Sam," he said, looking at her with eyes that pleaded for understanding. He stood up and followed her mother, leaving her to face Emilio who had his hand under his chin in an almost pensive gesture.

"I don't know what events you've set in motion, but you have some explaining to do," Samantha said, fuming.

Emilio sat back in the dining room chair, his one arm flung to the back while the other reached out for his wine. He looked almost predatory as he swirled the red liquid in his glass, before taking a sip. To be more accurate, he appeared to be the predator who already had his prey exactly where he wanted.

"You know why I'm here, Samantha. I'm here to take you back."

"Like hell!"

"You may want to hear me out before you're so quick to make decisions. Our story has long since developed into something that affects more than simply us alone."

"What do you mean?"

The stark look on his face conveyed an unsettling truth, one in which Emilio was already the victor. In the span of mere seconds, Samantha got the inkling that she had been blissfully ignorant of what had truly been happening in the backdrop of their relationship. All that time, she felt she was experiencing it.

"Years after we slipped away to Paris, our respective families met frequently to discuss how to best deal with the scandal. Somewhere in the breadth of those discussions, they formed a pact. It was a symbiotic relationship of sorts in the social circles they moved in, and both benefited in more ways than covering up the reasons for our sudden relocation. The Claremonts had a daughter on the line, and the Bianchis, a son. They were more influential together than they were apart."

"Our families have always done business," she remarked.

"My father has never saved another Hampton family from financial ruin."

The words made her go cold.

"Emilio, what are you playing at?"

"Perhaps," he said, as he leaned forward, "that is a question you should have asked your mother. She was after all the proprietor of one of your father's main businesses that she personally ran to the ground."

The chair she sat on screeched viciously as she stood up.

"I don't need to sit here listening to this." She walked around the table and then past him toward the living room, aiming for the porch that led out to the back. She flung the doors open, feeling the cool night air rush to meet her. But the heat was far from over. Emilio was right on her heel.

"You'd do well to listen!" he said, raising his voice. "Come to think of it, your mother would never in all her pride tell you this herself. So allow me to alleviate your ignorance. Her financial decisions cost them dearly in the long term. Predicting how this could compromise their fortune, my father negotiated with her to intervene, securing a debt from your family that runs far deeper than the bottom of their wallets. He saved their pride after all; that gleaming Claremont image that kept intact the esteem and reputation that means such a great deal to your kin."

"I renounced the family influence years ago Emilio. What does this have to do with us?" she asked through clenched teeth.

"Your actions were an insult to my family, after what they had done for yours. You walked away without consequence or retribution. It is something that cannot be overlooked. You may have left, but I never agreed for you to go. I want you back, and I *will* have you." His eyes glinted with that familiar possessiveness she had seen in their last years of being together. She was astounded how he was unable to see how it only drove her farther away from him.

"Ha! You sound like a child who has just found his plaything… Let me reiterate: I don't belong to you! Any story we may have had is finished."

"If that is your course of action, then believe me that the story is far from over. I have no doubt that this salacious bit on your family should cause quite an uproar among the community. You can avert that by atoning for what you have done."

"By taking you back?"

He smiled. It was the haunting kind of smile a criminal would give under interrogation. The kind of smile that spoke of full awareness of wrongdoing, but no remorse because of it.

"Little Sam…It is *I* that will be taking *you* back."

She walked up to him then, close enough to smell the heady cologne that drifted up from him. If the devil was as handsome as Emilio, a girl would succumb to his influence. Standing there, Samantha felt the opposite for once. "The ground you stand on is unstable, Bianchi. You're teetering on the edge of failure if you think your mind games are going to work on me this time."

"You're fairly confident, aren't you?"

"Of course I am. The mistakes of my parents have nothing to do with me personally. If that was your entry point of reestablishing our relationship, then I am sorry to disappoint you." She walked past him then, but he grabbed her by the arm. *There it was*, she thought. *The forcefulness. He isn't finished.*

"Then allow me to add another layer to this saga," he hissed. "Your mother's adultery."

She stopped fighting him then, her muscles going limp.

"W—what?"

"Hypocritical, don't you think? To pass the judgments on my family that you once did, while your own is by no means innocent. Allow me to elucidate to you the depth of secrecy your family has hidden, and how my family will use it against all of you if you don't play along."

Chapter 9:
Authority

The drive home was perilous, for no other reason besides the fact that she was trembling from both apprehension and anger.

Even though the road home had no traffic, she felt herself swerving more around the bends and braking suddenly as she mistook shadows for obstructions in the road. She couldn't recall how many times she simply stopped, feeling the rage quiver through her limbs to the erratic thump of her heart against her chest.

Samantha wanted nothing more than to be home. She wanted nothing more than to shut the door and close herself off from the world and its lingering threats—because there were many. And they all culminated into the irrefutable desires of Emilio Bianchi: once a lover, then a mistake, and now the villain.

But you liked that once, didn't you? she reprimanded herself. *Maybe you've always seen it, that volatile nature that's so intoxicating to a woman who'd known nothing but the boredom of safety in her life. You fell for the bad boy, and then he became too bad to handle.*

The journey home had taken her nearly two hours. It was almost midnight, and she breathed a sigh of relief as she pulled up to her house—possibly the last relief she would be experiencing for a while. She noticed too late the car parked in her driveway and the figure who climbed out.

God, Gareth. Not now. Please, not now.

But he waited for her as if he'd always be waiting. And she couldn't bear to lock her eyes with his as she climbed out of the car.

"Hey! I've been calling. I'm sorry, I know you were—"

"Gareth..." she interrupted. "I—I just can't...not right now, ok. I think—" She couldn't shape the words. They were there, ready in her mind, but her body refused to give them life. How did you draw away from the man you wanted to be close to you at the same time?

He must have seen the confusion in her eyes, before moving close to surround her with his arms. At his touch, she felt it then. The hot sting of tears before her eyes welled with the very emotions she was unable to express.

"I don't know what's going on," he whispered. "But we're going to go inside and you're going to tell me, alright?"

She didn't feel herself reacting, but he took something as an affirmation to lead her across the lawn and to the front door. Once inside, he sat her down, kneeling in front of her as he cupped her hand in the warmth of his own. She tried desperately to look for comfort in that gesture, but the turmoil of emotions inside her made his touch feel searing hot and she soon pulled her hands away to hug herself instead. He didn't protest as she withdrew into herself but kept a stalwart gaze locked on her face to search for any clue as to what she was going through.

He waited. He endured the storm of her silent uncertainty and patiently waited. He wouldn't relent. She never seemed to choose the men that ever gave up. He held his eyes on her, and eventually, she did react.

"Why are you here?" she blurted out, looking at him for the first time. She could tell it hurt. God knows she didn't mean it to, but the question came out sharp and confrontational. His eyes flinched even if the rest of him didn't and he stayed close to her—as close as she needed him to be, even though she was unfair toward him.

"It...it doesn't matter right now. You need—"

"It *does* matter. You weren't supposed to come tonight." Her manner was detached as if she had just canceled some business meeting. He kept his face neutral as he endured it, but he responded.

"A note had been left at my apartment building. On it was scribbled a number. I called, and received a warning from a voice I didn't recognize."

She leaned forward so suddenly that she startled him. She was certain that she must've looked frantic just then, but fear got the better of her.

"What did they say? *Tell me!*"

He frowned, trying to understand her reaction. "Sam, something is wrong here. Why are you—?"

"Dammit, Gareth. We're going in circles! Just tell me what the person on the other end of the line said to you."

He didn't react immediately, trying hard to get a read on her. Eventually, he relented, almost mumbling the words for fear of their power. *"Prima la famiglia."*

She sat back in her chair as the heart-wrenching silence that followed consumed her. "Gareth, you have to go..." she said, her voice cracking.

"The last time I walked away, I nearly missed a chance with you. I'm not making that mistake again."

"No, no...you don't have a choice. You have to leave here. You have to leave me. It's for your own good."

"I'm not going anywhere," he said as he sat himself down beside her. "You're going to tell me what happened tonight."

"Don't you understand?" she pleaded. "Do you know what those words mean? Those three simple words. It was a threat."

Any other man might have looked at her and thought she was crazy. The tone of her voice was nothing short of what it had once been so long ago when she was made to feel insane—also in her own home. She remembered herself back then. She resented that version of herself. Crippled by fear while looking over her shoulder; she had walked away from all of it thinking that her escape had been complete. What a fool she had been. Just a pretty little fool that thought she could melt back into the safety she once knew.

"I understand this much. The things we predicted to happen— the warning signs we noticed—they all connected faster than we were prepared for."

"For three years he bided his time. He waited until I wasn't watching before he chose to strike. He just needed the chess pieces to align in his favor. And now his own family has become pawns to his game. He even called you... He even had the *audacity* to call you so that he could cast the net of his threats wide enough."

"Sam, Emilio wasn't the one who called," Gareth commented. Her head spun toward him, and she stared at him with questioning eyes that mirrored his own.

"What do you mean? He must've. Who else could—"

"It was Abby, Sam."

She didn't register it at first, looking ahead of her into nothingness as she made room to organize her jumbled thoughts. Soon enough though, the scope of it all came crashing upon her mind. Abby...his ex, was a Bianchi. *Prima la famiglia*—family first.

"Oh my god. We're not just facing one of them anymore. They're all set against us."

"Sam, why did you believe Emilio was the person calling me?"

"Because he was there, at my parent's mansion."

His eyes went wide, and the light flashed over his lenses as his head tilted up in attention.

"Did he try anything to harm you?" There was a dangerous edge that started creeping into his voice, and she saw the vein bulging in his neck as his jaw went tense.

"No."

"Are you sure? Don't try to defend him, Sam," he nearly growled, "If he tried to touch you in any way..." He went quiet, visibly straining to compose himself.

"He didn't. There was a brief moment...when I *did* doubt what he'd do..." her voice was shaky then, and she didn't continue. She felt weak by the shock that the encounter had forced on her and she was digging deep to dry and combat it.

He stood up then, pulling his hand through his hair as he paced around for a while, looking almost stoic as he was facing his own inner demons. There were no words exchanged for a couple of minutes, as both of them reeled under the onslaught of the various deductions each of them were making.

"It isn't safe here," he said suddenly.

She looked up at him, imploring him for an answer with whatever look she could manage. A kind of numbness had overtaken her and she didn't feel in control of herself.

"Sam, I need you to pack a bag. Take what you need. Take anything that's important, even if it's remotely personal. I don't want you to leave anything behind that can be traced back to you."

His request seemed almost ridiculous. An entire house stretched out before them, filled with her belongings. But Samantha did look around, and the more she saw, the more it became less insane. Her house was nothing more than a minimalist Pinterest album that had been brought alive in a space she wanted to call home. Yet, in all the years she had never put up a picture. She had never placed anything on a shelf that was in any way sentimental. And nowhere, either on the back of a chair or on the floor—did she ever just leave something lying around. She treated her house more like a shelter than a living space. So, the more she looked around, the more alien that entire place suddenly became—void of any investment, memories, or anything personal.

As she snapped out of that self-inflicted spiral of thought, she noticed how he crouched to look underneath her furniture. He caught her eye then.

"Sam, go. Please. I want us to get out of here."

"Alright," she conceded. "But, what are you doing?"

"Looking for Meredith. Sure as hell we're not leaving her out of this."

***

The next few hours felt unreal.

His request to have her pack took more concentration than was necessary. In the end, she resorted to a capsule closet method of choosing the items to take along, while other essentials proved easier to recall.

Gareth did eventually find Meredith and proceeded to sweep through her home to gather other miscellanies that he figured shouldn't be lying around. As he fished out old tax reports, invoices, and even expired passports, she could not help but feel as though they were a pair of fugitives about to leave it all behind. A small part of those minutes had reminded her of another night, so similar and yet so different when she had packed a bag to leave with another man for an entirely different reason.

The drive took them just under an hour, and they were back in Gareth's flat. She thought how funny it was, that the last time they were here they had only premeditated—and perhaps underestimated—the threat posed to them by Emilio Bianchi.

But she still hadn't told Gareth the entirety of it all. He also didn't venture to ask on the drive. He just assumed by her reaction alone that Emilio wasn't just being difficult, but dangerous.

"Don't unpack. We'll be leaving early morn—" Looking at his watch, he caught himself. "Well, later in fact."

"Again?"

"Yeah. For now, I just wanted us to get out of that house. Here at least, I figured we'd be safe for the night. But I want us to put even more distance between us and the drama that is unfolding on this end."

"Where would we be headed?"

"Maine."

"Maine?" The shock was momentary, but the more she considered it in light of the current circumstances, the more it dissipated. "I guess—I guess we have to, yeah."

"Sam, I know things are heated right now. I just put two and two together and figured we're in danger. However, I need you to tell me exactly what Emilio said to you when you went over to your parents."

Samantha sat down, pulling her hair back until she held it against her neck. Breathing deeply, she tried to organize the different parts of the story in her own mind. "When Emilio and I were in Paris, our families underwent a string of negotiations to deal with the apparent scandal that our decision to elope had caused. Allegedly, it had many social repercussions that we never saw. You have to understand—though, I think you do— that these people, the upper crust of society, are hardwired differently than we are. The status quo means everything to them, and it's their aim to maintain it."

"They've tied their self-worth to external validations."

"That's right. Emilio was an eligible bachelor back in the day. If anything, there was nothing his father wanted more than to have him acquire an auspicious match to secure the legacy."

"But, Emilio had an older brother from what I could remember."

"He did. But Stefano is gay."

"Ah. So essentially, a lot rode on Emilio."

"Exactly. Which is why his parents weren't too fond of his choices. However, I didn't know that my mother had similarly been grooming me for one of these matches as well. God, it's so Victorian in principle...these cunning arrangements that are never forced, but strongly implied and favored." She wiped her hands across her face, catching a breath before she continued. "When Lorenzo, Emilio's father, found out that it was a Claremont he eloped with, he foresaw a way to re-enter the sphere of influence over his son's life. The two families struck a negotiation—a bond that secured their mutual interests and acted as a contingency should any of them be in trouble. It was the kind of deal that you didn't seal with signatures. As Bianchis began attending the parties thrown by the Claremonts and vice versa, people soon got whiff of this unspoken alliance."

"So it was all an impression created through social tactics?"

"Most of these things are."

"How did this have bearing on the two of you?"

"It didn't. At least not immediately. Neither of us cared much for the way our reputations would have been tarnished back home. But our families did and altered the story of our absence from the Hampton circles with their version. They had ulterior motives obviously, and a marriage between Samantha Claremont and Emilio Bianchi inevitably implied an alliance between my father and his. Only, the real fulcrum behind all of this was *my mother...*"

"Your father never knew then..."

"Not truly. He wasn't stupid. Just ignorant. He would see the company at club gatherings enriched by Lorenzo and his kin, but like any Bianchi, the man had a way to tell a story that even my father was misled by as to their true motives for even being there. It was all a show, but I think Lorenzo was surveying the battlefield with every social event he attended."

"Just like his brother."

She didn't know who was talking about immediately, but she soon recalled the name Vincenzo. As the name settled on her mind, so did another memory.

"Oh my God, Gareth! Your 'adoptive' father...he is the middle brother to Lorenzo.... That means Abby—"

"Is Emilio's cousin. I think that on that first night I met your ex, there was more than just a standoff between two men going on their usual power-trips."

Wow. A man owning up to his games. You don't see that a lot. She was surprised she could even feel amused by something so silly, given the circumstances.

"You recognized each other, didn't you?"

"I think we did. *I* did. And I suddenly recalled Emilio...even as a kid. We never talked about it. We probably should have. But I just felt that he had occupied enough of our mental real estate that one night. I wanted to focus on us." He gave her a sad kind of smile, which she returned.

"I get it. I wanted the same."

"So, if this 'brotherhood,' for lack of a better word, was never placed in writing, then what is their leverage? Are we just outrunning a bunch of psychos with attachment issues? An alliance of our exes, of sorts? Or is there more?"

"There's more," she answered softly. "Lorenzo's leverage was sealed with two distinct factors. The first was an overzealous business decision my mother had made. She had made multiple property investments in new developments like Meadowbrook Pointe, in East Meadow, Country Pointe in Plainview, and even put some money into the Aman New York Residences. She was rather secretive of this, as some of their main sources of traditional income had dried up and she couldn't afford it. So, riding the family name to carry favor with their bank manager, she acquired a number of home loans that allowed her to make these investments. It was a decision that would have many repercussions. Those consequences finally came to bite her in the ass when the bank manager's generosity of approving such loans prompted a review. Ultimately, the payments on those properties were adjusted and additional penalties were applied. The economy wasn't doing great at the time either, and so interest rates rose exponentially, and my mother saddled up an increasing debt that they couldn't afford to pay off. Not without a significant cut in their fortune. She wanted to keep this from my father, you see."

He sat down on one of the couches across from her, and the leather creaked ominously as he sank into his seat. He wiped his hand over his mouth while staring into open space, and she knew he was making the right connections. "Tell me she didn't approach the Bianchi's for money."

"She did. Daphne Claremont would never suffer at the hands of shame. Lorenzo...sweet, conniving, generous Lorenzo, did have the funds to save her out of the financial ruin she had secured for herself. That intervention of the transfer of funds was exactly the written leverage he needed to be sure that their alliance turned into a situation where the Claremonts were indebted to them. Of course, he didn't want the money back. He didn't need it. He wanted loyalty. With his son and her daughter tied to one another, all the cards were in his favor."

"But there was one flaw in his reasoning. You and Emilio were never married."

"No. But he assumed we were. Actually, I think Emilio lied to him about it."

"Emilio confessed all of this to you...at the dinner."

"Yes."

"I don't understand. Why would he lie to his father then if he is soliciting Lorenzo's help to get his way?"

"Because that lie was told years ago. I have no doubt that they have worked hard to reconcile many truths. Emilio's illicit dealings before that were just of such a severe degree that he couldn't afford to reach out for family help unless he wished to pull his father right into the cesspool of his problems."

"It means that Emilio must have tied any loose ends in Paris to even be brazen enough to return. It freed him once again to recruit the help of the illustrious Bianchi influence."

Samantha nodded. "Lorenzo never knew the reason for my return. Somehow, the blasé nature of the rich affords them the luxury to never ask many questions. I think in his mind, he believed that Emilio and I simply split. He didn't know that I just left."

"But you're still not married, Sam. There is no hold over you."

"I—I don't know. There must be. I still don't think Lorenzo knows the truth. I think he came back to tell his father that we're still married and that I'm the wife that simply walked out without ever thinking to file for divorce."

"So the hold he thinks he has...is all based on the shared pride he thinks you have in the Claremont reputation? Rich families go through financial turmoil all the time. Surely your—" He stopped short then, and she knew he must have been unfolding the bigger picture in his mind. They both knew the issue was more complex merely by the fact that they were dealing with a Bianchi.

"If this were to come out, it would only be the first blow to the Claremont name. By virtue of the fact that I am back in New York, any business ties I may have had would be brought into question as well. Like it or not, this impacts my career. This impacts my entire life here, purely on the basis that people buy into salacious stories and make anyone tied to it victims of a devil-horns effect."

"You said it's only the first blow. So...there's more."

"Yes. Jesus, I—" her voice broke, and she suddenly felt extremely fragile. Gareth was next to her then, cradling her on his lap as the emotion took her suddenly.

"Sam, it's ok. You're not alone. Please. You need to tell me. Let me share the burden with you."

"It's bad, Gareth. It's really bad," she got out. "My mother...she—she cheated on my dad."

She could feel his muscles tense, before he said, "Tell me."

"For years, she had an on-and-off affair with—with Lorenzo's youngest brother—Emmanuel."

She heard the sharp intake of breath from him then. It made her sit upright. His face was drained of color, and it immediately made her eyes dry up as she became more alert. "What?"

"Sam...Emmanuel has been in prison for the last four years. He was charged with attempted manslaughter."

She must have mimicked his response then. A chill ran down her spine. It was another piece to a puzzle that was becoming increasingly complicated.

"Did—did he tell you when this relationship ended?"

"No. But he did say the Bianchi's shunned him after that. I just never asked him why."

"Oh god," Gareth said, in an almost desolate voice. "Sam, I've long suspected what most people must have been thinking; that the Bianchi's are inevitably part of the Italian Mafia. The running story from the inside, when I was still with Abby, was that Emmanuel tried to overthrow one of the family dons in a coup—some other influential cousin. The person in question...God, I wish I could remember his name...was somewhere in France at the time. He— wait...Emilio. He was in Paris."

"You don't think....?"

"That he is somehow connected to all of this? I wouldn't be surprised. If he was, then your ex was better at evading the hellfire that rained down on him whenever he attracted attention. It also means he is a duplicitous bastard that was using his family while perhaps even working against them."

Sam felt incapable of sitting down a moment longer. Her hands tangled in her hair as she pressed in on her head as if to bring some stability to the wild thoughts that were running through her haphazardly. "My mother's involvement with Emmanuel...she must have known. She must have known all of it."

Gareth gave a nervous laugh. Sam swung around to see a nervous expression on his face as he looked wide-eyed into space. He seemed to do that often as he got lost in his train of thought. "It's crazy. Wouldn't it be funny...? No, not funny. Strange, almost coincidental, if your mother knew all about the coup. If she knew all about the involvement of Emilio in the plot. What if Emilio was the one to move in? To calm the position? That would inevitably make him close to invincible...including you. What if she did this all for you?"

The tears came then, flowing down her face in torrents. She cupped her mouth with her hand to stop the wracking sobs from escaping her body.

"Sam! God, I'm sorry! I didn't mean to upset you. That was insensitive. I didn't think." He went to her and pulled her in an embrace. And she cried into him, finally succumbing to the shock and the immensity of it all. She wasn't mad at Gareth, even if all his observations were overwhelming to process. The worst of it was that his entire theory, with all its interwoven details that made it border on a conspiracy, was plausible. He simply held her, tightening the hold as he felt the emotion surge through her.

"If—Gareth if something like that were to ever come out…"

"Then it can cause a hell of a lot of trouble."

And what both of them knew, in that instant, was that Emilio was the authority to this perfect little blackmail. *He had bided his time*, the thought echoed in her mind. *Now he has us all.*

Chapter 10:
Disobedience

Neither of them slept much.

Instead, they spilled their feelings into the longing embrace of each other's bodies. There, in Gareth's arms, she felt safe. In the moment where all her certainties wavered, the solidity of his form against her made her crave him all the more. The sensation was primal as she pulled him closer every time he was on top of her. There was a desperation riding on the timbre of every moan. A silent wish for more rode the exhalation of every breath. Fire danced under fingertips wherever it touched his skin, raking across his back as he thrust harder, and faster. All the tensions melted away into sweet seductive raptures that they created that night until they lay spent in the silent aftermath of having spoken volumes without saying a single word.

She would go anywhere with him then. There was a magnetic pull to him through his resolute demeanor as the dawn broke. He made calls, the content of which was a mystery to her as she heard the hiss of whispers traveling to and from as he paced. She didn't need to know. She didn't want to know. To some extent, she even thought it was for the best. The less she knew the better, for the less compromised they would ultimately be.

Emilio's threats hinged off one important variable: knowing where Samantha was. If he couldn't find her, there was no way for him to plot the next best move on his malicious little gameboard.

When she finished packing, she simply looked at Meredith. The cat had adapted fairly quickly to her new surroundings, even seeming more lively than usual. In this twisted little game, her presence seemed to be the only thing that didn't seem as mangled. It lent a strange sense of normality to their situation. And with it, hope.

That hope seemed to shrink then, like the retreating light from the entrance of a tunnel, as she heard Gareth's voice raise in disparaging shouts over the phone. His free hand was clenched in a fist by his side, and his entire body seemed coiled as if ready for a fight.

He swung around then, with the dual look of panic and anger playing on his expression. "We have to leave here, now!"

"What happened?" she urged.

"The building manager said that one of the security guards had seen Abby in the vicinity as he was driving this way to relieve his partner on night duty."

"I know this is a silly question, but it isn't just coincidence?"

"No, I'm afraid not. Abby lives in Brooklyn. There is no reason for her to be in Queens this early in the morning. Besides, I've known her for years. She ran her business from home. There's no need for her to travel around this much. Something's up. I'm not sticking around a moment longer to find out."

"I'm ready," she said, hoping he could hear the dedication she tried to push into that comment.

"Good. Head down to the foyer with your bags. I'll catch Meredith and be right behind you."

"Don't you want me to catch her? She's my responsibility."

"Nope. Besides, I can tell she's taken to me more," he winked, trying to lighten the mood. "Now go," he said firmly.

She complied and dragged the part of her life that she could fit into two suitcases down to the lower level. Beyond the front entrance, she could see the flash of cars falling into the stream of the early morning NYC hustle. She had a clear view of corner cafés across the street as well, already opening their doors to patrons who had come to conduct their early morning business.

Gareth was taking longer than expected. She wrapped her arms around herself, trying to rub away the dread that settled on her skin in a million pin-pricks. Her eyes were still fixed outside, drawn suddenly to the confident strut of a lone figure who stopped outside of Dali's Corner. Fierce high-heel ankle boots were fitted on the end of legs that seemed to go on forever before they reached a black leather miniskirt tied with a thin belt. A tie-neck raglan sleeve blouse wrapped the bodice in burgundy. Her short feathered hairstyle was a hundred devil horns that simply pointed in different directions, framing sharp cheekbones and a prominent nose that dominated her face. Her lips, full and slightly pouted, carried the sneer that only a trained eye could see. Her eyes would have completed the story if not hidden behind oversized sunglasses. But perhaps that was intentional, lest the mystery be revealed.

She realized how long she must've looked at the figure judging how far she actually was from it. The side street onto which the side entrance of the building opened was small, but two lanes still divided them from the other side. Her eyes strained from the concentration, but something about the woman drew her attention with such absolution that she couldn't look away. And then *he* came.

Dashing and menacing as ever, Emilio walked up the street. The woman gave a short-half smile as she noticed him. He reached her then, planting kisses on both cheeks before drawing her into an embrace that he only ever reserved for a few people. She saw it then, perhaps in their way of being together or the similarities in their features, but the realization hit her with such inquietude that she felt as if the world was spinning around her.

Samantha couldn't explain how she knew it was Abby, but she was certain of it then as she was of anything in her life. Two lethal vipers had sailed over the street to meet one another to poison any hope they may have had of a getaway.

Another feeling struck her then. It hailed fire onto her sense of trepidation, beating back the crippling fear to make room for a wave of searing anger. *How dare they?* she mused, filling the thought with such fury that she was certain they must have felt it on some cosmic level. *Who are these entitled scum to fuck with other people's lives? As if each one of us who isn't a Bianchi are mere playthings to satiate their needs.*

She felt a hand land on her shoulder then, a featherlight touch as long dexterous fingers grazed ever so gently to get her attention. She turned around to see Gareth then, his eyes fixed on where hers had been but a moment ago. "They were closer than we thought."

"What are we going to do?" she asked, with a voice far stronger than she thought she was capable of.

"I wanted to leave this way, but there is still another route by which to get to my car. They won't see us if we're careful."

"Lead the way."

The foyer had two exits, one which opened onto the side street they'd been looking at and another leading to the main street out front where traffic pulsed in relentless movement. Gareth's route took them through a door only used by the tenants, leading to basement parking that opened further up onto the side street from where their watchers lie in wait.

"My car is parked out on the street, to the left. They're further up the street on the right. It's a metallic dark grey Audi A4 Avant."

"That's...not a car I've ever seen you drive before."

"No, it isn't. I had it switched last night with some help from a contact. Now, listen to me. When you turn left, don't turn your back. Don't look around until you reach the trunk of the car. Open it immediately and toss your bag in. Here, take Meredith. I'll deal with your other suitcase. Once your things are inside, throw the cat on the backseat and climb in. Alright?"

"Yeah." She pulled a strand of her hair back behind her ear, uncertain whether she should ask what she wanted to. "That...that's her, isn't it? Abby?"

He sighed and nodded once. She didn't ask any other questions. Taking one bag and the cat cage, she made her way up the ramp and onto the street. Her heart pounded as she turned left, and as if feeling her mother's worry, even Meredith started to protest. Sam wished she would stay quiet. She had never been so self-aware in her life, and her legs felt wobbly as she tried to hurry to get to the car he'd pointed out. It was hard, in that jungle of grey and concrete, but she found her quarry and felt herself calm as her fingers closed over the cool metallic latch.

She opened it and lifted in her suitcase. She placed the cat on the backseat and then found herself in the front passenger's seat where she counted her breaths, waiting for the sound of the trunk to close. It finally came after she felt a weight land in the back. Next was the ruffle of fabric on the driver's seat next to her as Gareth climbed in. He seemed to exhale a breath he'd been holding forever, simply holding the steering wheel as he stared out through the windshield. She noticed all of this in her periphery. Her own neck felt stiff as her gaze was drawn forward, almost expectant that something was to hit them from the front.

The engine awoke and brought them out of their spellbound anxiety, and some relief began to set in as he turned the car around and headed up the street. The moment of truth came upon them as they edged slowly past the café. She willed every fiber of her being not to look in the direction, but as the car crept past over the last few inches before reaching the end of the street, the compulsion overtook her.

She saw him, the man she once loved, sitting just inside. His face was the mimicry of everything a woman ever wanted, of everything a man ever wanted to be, and of everything the devil could never accomplish.

Look at me! her mind shouted his way. *Look at me, you conniving coward!* She wanted nothing more at that moment. She wanted nothing more for him to see her in that car, driving away, slipping through his fingers while he believed he was setting an entire plot in motion to win her back.

But Emilio never did raise his eyes. Emilio never did notice as his most coveted prize was moving away from him. Pride had always been his greatest downfall. All he ever could see was right in front of him—a means to an end. This time it was the shape of his venomous cousin who seemed to play on the edge of lunacy. *I wonder what she sees. Maybe she never had blinders at all. Maybe she always saw too much and never knew what to do with it.* They were the perfect archetypes for the disillusioned powerful—with sights too narrow or scopes too wide. They were always prisoners, kept in place by the bonds of their own dark desire.

Samantha never got the satisfaction to stand witness to Emilio's chagrin. But as space opened up in the main traffic and they turned out of the side street to slip inside it, none of it even seemed to matter.

She wasn't sure what the future held or how they would face the approaching storm. For the time being, however, they were driving into the eye of it. And as Gareth placed his hand over her own, offering a reassuring smile that promised things that even he could not predict past their uncertainties, she could not help but feel that they'd endure...

...without the help of a family legacy.

PETIT TRAITÉ

MATHÉMATIQUE ET PRATIQUE

DES

OPÉRATIONS COMMERCIALES

ET

FINANCIÈRES

PAR

J. PATOU

Agrégé des Sciences Mathématiques, Professeur au Lycée de Tunis.

II

ÉLÉMENTS D'ALGÈBRE FINANCIÈRE

PARIS

VUIBERT ET NONY, ÉDITEURS

63, Boulevard Saint-Germain, 63

1905